I0719169

Kiss:
Frog Prince Retold

DEMELZA CARLTON

A tale in the Romance a Medieval Fairy Tale series

Lost Plot Press

ISBN-13: 978-1-925799-24-8

ISBN-10: 1-925799-24-7

DEDICATION

For all those who've kissed too many frogs along the
way to happily-ever-after.

One

If Philemon never felt the scorching desert sands beneath his feet again, he would be a happy man. "How much further?" he demanded.

The camel driver turned and bowed apologetically. "At least half the night, Your Highness. If you had not decreed a slower pace, we would be there already."

"Perhaps, but I would have left my blackened balls somewhere in the desert, for they would have bounced off at the pace this beast was going before."

Philemon heard sniggering from behind him, but it was hard to discern one man from another, silhouetted against the setting sun and all. Ah, let them laugh. He'd served with the guardsmen until his father had died, forcing him to assume the throne.

Philemon continued, "There's little point taking one of the Sultan's daughters as my bride if I cannot consummate the marriage on our wedding night. If I cannot give the city an heir, you'll find yourself a new Prince of Tasnim, I am certain of it!"

The laughter was louder now, for they all knew as well as he did that he was the last of his father's line, and they'd need to look outside the city walls to find someone of sufficiently royal blood to take his place. Whether they liked Philemon or not, he was still their prince, a man of Tasnim.

Which was why he gave the orders, not the camel driver. "We must set up camp, rest for the night, and we will reach Tasnim on the morrow," Philemon finished.

"But there is no water, Your Highness," the camel driver protested.

Philemon fought to keep his temper. Did the camel driver think he was blind? "I can see that," he said with forced calm. "Take us to the nearest oasis, and we will camp there."

The camel driver spluttered. "But…Your Highness…the nearest oasis was the one we left this morning. The only water for miles is in the wells of Tasnim itself, unless some magical wadi appears before us."

Philemon laughed, but not for long. The man's idea of magic had merit. Philemon rubbed his ring, the one symbol of his sovereignty he carried with him everywhere.

The djinn appeared, bowing low. "What do you wish, Master?"

"Make me an oasis here," Philemon commanded.

The djinn snorted with laughter. "My master jests. The best I can make for you is a puddle, if I drink a good skin of wine and piss on that rock." He tugged at the loincloth he wore, as if he intended to do just that.

"I need water for my men and the camels to

drink. Now," Philemon insisted.

The djinn spread his arms wide. "I have told you what I can do. Maybe you should have found yourself a different djinn, someone more powerful who can command water instead of stone. Fat lot of good he'd be, when it comes to opening the gates of Tasnim, but he might be able to fetch you a drink."

A different djinn. And Philemon had such a thing. "Fetch the genie of the lamp. The one you found in the oasis outside the city gates," he said. "I have a task for him."

A servant appeared, bowed, then offered Philemon the dented, tarnished bronze lamp. Philemon rubbed his thumb across what appeared to be a scorch mark on the scored surface. Back and forth, back and forth…until blue smoke began to stream from the lamp's spout.

The enormous djinn abased himself on the sand. "How may I serve you, Master?"

"Make me an oasis right here, big enough to quench the thirst of every man and beast here twice over, and still have enough water for me to bathe," Philemon ordered. He waited for this djinn to say the same words as the servant of the ring.

"Your wish is my command, Master. It shall be done."

And for that moment, Philemon knew he was the most powerful man in the desert.

Two

Anahita knew the very moment she lost her sense of fear. One moment, she was screaming, her broken arm splintering into a million needles of pain to the unholy delight of her new husband, and the next, the whole world went silent.

He would beat her to death tonight, whether by accident or design, her dreamy mind told her. She should have been afraid, but death would be an improvement over the endless round of beatings that inevitably ended in rape. Her father had given her to this man in an attempt to bring peace, but Sheikh Fakhri did not understand the meaning of the word. He attacked her father's people to capture women to replace his dwindling number of wives, and he beat her every time her father's men fought back.

The only way to end this was to stop him.

The sheikh cupped his hardening manhood and grinned.

No. She would not submit to him tonight, or any other night. If she was going to die, she would do so without that final indignity.

Anahita dragged herself to her feet. "You're a coward, a man whose only courage comes from beating women. I hope when my father's men cut you down, they feed your body to pigs. Female pigs," she said.

He shouted for his guards, and two enormous men rushed into the tent.

Anahita knew them both – men the sheikh had assigned to watch her so that she did not run away.

"Hold her down, so that I can cut out her lying tongue," he ordered, and the men moved toward her.

Anahita had one chance. "Don't touch my arm. It's broken," she implored, cradling it to her chest. Her husband might be a monster, but these two were merely men.

The guards looked uncertain. A moment's hesitation was all she needed. She crumpled forward, righting herself just before she fell, feeling the leather hilt of her salvation in her good hand.

She might die tonight, but she would not die alone. She lunged.

The guard's blade pierced Fakhri's throat, and Anahita thrust it in deeper, before ripping it out. Fakhri fell to his knees, clutching his gaping throat, but the lifeblood sheeting down his chest told the tale's end for him as he gasped his last.

When the light went out of his eyes, he pitched over sideways, his limp dick flopping onto the tent floor.

He would violate no houris in the afterlife, either, Anahita vowed, putting her borrowed blade to work again. She threw the pieces of hacked-off gristle onto a brazier, while blood leaked sluggishly from his groin.

Only then did she turn to face the guards. Without fear, for if she died tonight, she died victorious. She held out the bloodied blade, but it slipped from her hand, to land point-down in the sand.

Powerless. That's what she was now. That's all she had ever been.

"Do your worst," she said, falling to her knees. But she kept on falling, into darkness that rose up to claim her.

Three

The final stage of the journey home seemed to take hardly any time at all, or perhaps that was because Philemon spent most of it wondering what he would call his new oasis. After all, it was his – created at his command – so he should have the pleasure of naming it.

His first thought was the most obvious name for the place, but calling it Lake Philemon wasn't enduring enough. Philemon was hardly a rare name, even for a prince, and he wanted no confusion in anyone's mind that the oasis belonged to the Prince of Tasnim.

But to call it Tasnim Oasis implied that it belonged to the whole city, instead of its ruler. It was true that the wealth of water it contained would belong to the people of the city who travelled outside the city walls, for it was within his territory, but…the Lake of the People took away from the magic of making water appear in the desert.

Well, the djinn had performed the magic, but no one wanted the place named after a slave. Even if Philemon had known the slave's name, which of course he did not. There were far more important people for him to remember.

Including Fadi, his vizier, who was waiting for him in his apartments when Philemon arrived back in Tasnim.

Philemon sighed. He would have preferred his concubines to be waiting for him, but they would have to wait. The city came first, before Philemon's desires.

"I trust the city continued to prosper under your care?" Philemon asked, beckoning for a servant to bring refreshments for himself and the vizier.

Fadi bowed. "I do my best, as always, Your Highness. The city has endured under your family's rule and enjoyed good fortune for many years as a result. But a strange thing happened this morning..." He accepted a cup of wine and sipped from it.

Philemon paused to savour the first taste of a particularly fine vintage, before he replied, "Ah, this is Tasnim. Did a cat chase a dog? Did my jewelled garden grow? Or did a bird fly out of a well?"

Fadi managed a smile, but it did not reach his eyes. "I fear it is nothing so small as a bird, Your Highness."

Philemon felt the first twinge of unease in his belly. "Then spit it out. Tell me what has befallen my city, so that I may set things to rights."

"It's the wells, my prince. Yesterday, they were fine, but this morning, none of the buckets would reach the water."

"Then they need more rope! I am certain there is plenty in the storerooms. Have someone fetch it and the wells will soon be set to rights. Perhaps the ladies of Tasnim have bathed more often of late, or this summer has been a thirstier season than most." Philemon forced himself to smile, even as a chill crept around his heart. Water was life, and the lifeblood of Tasnim. If something happened to their water supply…

"I already have, Your Highness. It took a dozen yards of rope, but we struck water again." Fadi swallowed, as if he hesitated to say more.

Philemon knew his vizier, for the man had loyally served his father for longer than Philemon could remember. He waited in silence.

Finally, Fadi continued, "I set my clerks to search the records, looking for reports of this ever happening before. So far…they have found nothing. The waters of Tasnim have never dropped by so much. Ever. I fear…magic, or some sort of curse. Forgive me, my prince, but have you somehow angered someone powerful in your trip to the capital? Through some small act, insignificant to you…aroused the enmity of some sorcerer?"

Philemon burst out laughing. "Fadi, I visited the Sultan for one purpose alone: to secure a wife from among his daughters. His matchmaker assured me that the Sultan finds favour with my proposal, and will send an appropriate girl as soon as I send word we are ready for her. Unless some sorcerer has set his heart on the same girl the Sultan intends to give me – chosen by the Sultan, not me, for surely he knows his daughters best – I cannot imagine what offence I have given anyone. And if I have…why, let them come! They may bring an army to Tasnim's gates, and we shall stand, as we always have, undefeated."

Fadi returned his smile. "Perhaps you are right, my prince. Maybe the earthquake we felt last night is the reason for it. It shook dust from the ceilings, and spilled soup from my bowl, but little else. Perhaps the water beneath the city spilled out of its vessel, too."

"That's the spirit. Tasnim will not fall while men like us rule her!"

Fadi left soon after, and Philemon headed to the garden, where his favourite concubines waited among the jewelled trees. The sound of soft music and feminine laughter lifted his spirits like nothing else.

Yet later, when both he and his concubines were sated, he dismissed them back to the harem, and lay alone in the darkness with his thoughts.

Tasnim would not fall, he swore to himself. He was the prince of this city, and he would defend it to his dying breath.

He padded out to where his bags had been brought in, and dug out the dented lamp. When the djinn appeared, Philemon didn't give him time to ask for orders. "I command you to fill the wells of Tasnim to where they were before I left the city," he said.

The djinn eyed him. "You want me to bring the water back?"

Philemon swore. "You stole the water from our wells? Then yes, I do want you to bring it back! Immediately!"

"I hear and obey," the djinn said, and vanished.

Satisfied, Philemon headed back to bed, and a peaceful night's sleep.

It would be the last peace he would know

for a long, long time.

Four

"Just leave her, and let's go!" a male voice hissed.

Pain stabbed through Anahita's arm again — that's what had woken her — and she whimpered, her throat too hoarse to scream. She forced her eyes open, but the hulking shadow bending over her blocked the light. The only thing she could be certain of was that he was the one hurting her.

"Stop," she croaked, batting at him with her good arm.

"When I have bandaged this properly, or

you will be crippled for the rest of your life," the man said.

Anahita blinked and turned her head to get a better look at what he was doing. True to his word, he was bandaging her arm, which was already splinted so that it would heal straight.

"Take me home, where it will not matter. Servants will take care of me," she said.

The men exchanged a glance. "Your home is probably destroyed like ours was, and every other village Fakhri attacked. Your home is gone."

"Haidar, we have to go. Leave her. She will only slow us down." The second man glanced around nervously. "They'll blame us for this. We cannot be here when the body is found!"

"And where will we go? Our home is no more, cousin. If we leave her, she will surely die, for Fakhri's men are no better than he is. I will not leave her to pay the price for justice for Nasrin. She deserves better."

"Take me home to the capital. Tell the Sultan about Fakhri. He must know," Anahita insisted. She grabbed the first man – Haidar's – arm and heaved herself to her feet. Up she went…and down again, too, for her legs would not hold her. But she would not give up. She eyed the tent wall, and the inch-wide gap between it and the sand. Fakhri's tent stood at the edge of camp, where fewer people would be disturbed by the screams of his women. For once, this would work in her favour.

She grabbed the jewelled cup Fakhri had swilled wine from and used it to shovel sand away from the tent wall. Soon enough, she'd dug a dent big enough for her to squirm through. "If we go this way, and keep to the shadows, we can reach the camels without anyone seeing us. Do you know where they keep supplies? We'll need food and water – it's a long journey."

"Well, you heard the lady," the second man said. He threw himself into the shallow ditch Anahita had created, and after some widening of the pit, managed to leave the tent. "Come, cousin. Freedom awaits."

Haidar eyed Anahita. "What do they do to escaped slaves in your city, lady? Is it worse than what the desert people do to murderers?"

Anahita wet her lips. "I do not know,

but…but…if you are the Sultan's subjects, then surely he will free you for bringing word of what Fakhri did to your village. I swear I will do everything I can to see you freed, for you should never have been slaves in the first place."

"I will take a small chance of life over none at all. You first, lady, and I will follow after," Haidar said.

Anahita nodded, and followed Haidar's cousin. She hissed in pain as her broken ribs protested at bearing her weight, but she did not stop. She could not make it back home alone, and these men could help her.

When she reached the cool night air, Anahita forced herself to her feet, ignoring the pain and the swirling in her head. If she showed weakness now, they would leave her behind. So she gritted her teeth, and headed for the camels.

A heavy hand landed on her shoulder, yanking her back. "What are you doing?" he hissed.

Anahita glared at him. "If we want to get out of here, we'll need a distraction to hold their attention. Releasing the camels to stampede through the camp should do it."

"Or a fire," Haidar said cheerfully, rubbing his hands together as he rose to his feet.

A wisp of smoke curled up from the tunnel they'd crawled through.

"Fool!" Haidar's cousin growled. "I'll get us some supplies. You get her to the camels. If she's not there when I get back, we go without her!" He darted off.

"Shall we?" Haidar asked.

Anahita nodded, and led the way to the camels on the outskirts of the camp. She selected four who had been part of her entourage when she arrived, and led them away from the rest. "Stay here with him," she told them, pointing at Haidar. To him, she said, "These were my father's. They will carry us home." Then she untied the rest. "There is food hidden in the tents, with the men," she said. "Trample the tents and you will find it, but hurry!"

Heads lifted, and they stared at her uncertainly for a moment.

"Food. The men in the camp, the ones who

beat you, they are hiding it!" she said. "Go and get it!"

A cloud of sand surrounded her, as the grunting beasts rose to their full height, then lumbered off toward the camp to wreak havoc. Screams erupted. The screams of men, not women, for once.

"Yes," she whispered, elated.

"What did you do?" Haidar demanded.

A shriek sliced through the sandstorm. A sound Anahita recognised. "Vega!" She ran toward her.

"Come back here, girl!"

Haidar's hand reached for her, but Anahita dodged and ran on. She could not leave Vega here. But in the dark, the eagle's tethers were impossible to untie.

"Give me your knife," she said, holding out her hand.

"We need to go back to get Asad," Haidar said.

"I'm not leaving Vega. She is my hunting falcon, and she's coming home with me." Anahita glared at him. "Give me your knife, and help me cut the others free. They will help with the distraction."

She felt the cold hilt in her hand, and closed her fingers around it. The sharp blade sliced through Vega's jesses, and the bird rose into the air with a triumphant shriek.

"You may hunt in the morning. For now, stay with me," Anahita told the eagle, who settled obediently on her shoulder. She made quick work of the other birds' restraints, too.

The other birds eyed Vega warily, not budging from their perches for fear of what the eagle might do to them.

"Attack the men. They keep you prisoner. Once you are free, you may hunt, and all your prey will belong to you, and no one else. I will keep you safe from this eagle," Anahita told the birds. "Fly!"

The falcons rose, a mismatched flock with one deadly purpose. Vega clicked her beak in frustration, and Anahita reached up to stroke the eagle's feathers. "You will fly free at dawn, I promise. But we must get far from here."

She hurried back to the camels, where both men stood, waiting.

"What did you do?" Haidar asked. "I've

never seen animals obey like that."

Anahita smiled. "Magic."

"You're a witch?" Haidar's eyes showed white with fear.

"What's that bird for?" Asad asked, pointing at the eagle.

"Vega is what you would call my familiar. My friend." Her only friend out here.

"She'd better not scare the camels," Asad said, climbing onto the lead animal.

Anahita chose the smallest camel and struggled to climb onto her back. Between her broken arm and Vega, she was exhausted as she sank into the saddle.

"A drink for you, lady, for we will not have time to stop until we reach the next oasis," Haidar said, passing her a water skin.

Anahita nodded her thanks, uncorked it, and drank.

Wine coated her tongue, a welcome wetness as it trickled down her raw throat. Then she tasted the bitterness behind it, and it was too late. She tried to curse, but the words wouldn't come.

The opium stole her wits and darkness

engulfed her again.

<h1 style="text-align:center">Five</h1>

Day after day, the water level dwindled, despite Philemon ordering the djinn to refill the wells every night. One well ran dry, then another, and what had once been whispers became loud enough for even the prince to hear his citizens' concerns.

Philemon summoned the djinn door guardian. "What do you know about the other djinn?" he asked him.

The djinn shrugged. "He is the slave of a lamp, like I am the servant of your ring of office. He's powerful enough, but I don't trust him. My treason has long since passed into legend, but what is his crime? What did he do to deserve eternal enslavement? What if he is here to serve some other master, who wishes to bring Tasnim low?"

"You're right. I don't trust him either. Every night, I have ordered him to rectify our water woes, and every morning, they are worse. What does one do when a djinn is not following his master's orders?" Philemon asked.

The djinn shook his head. "I have never heard of such a thing. It should not be possible. He must be in service to someone else who means you and the city ill. Someone whose orders are more powerful than your own. The only permitted reason for refusing an order is because a djinn lacks the power to do what he's asked. Otherwise, I would fill the city's wells myself, but you know I cannot."

"So what do you suggest?" Philemon couldn't believe he was asking the djinn for help, but this djinn was once a vizier as loyal to the city as Fadi. And who knew djinn better than one of them?

"You can only fight magic with magic, and you need the help of someone more powerful than the lamp slave. I can let it be known among magical circles that you are looking for the help of a powerful enchantress, and you are willing to pay a high price for it."

It was on the tip of Philemon's tongue to ask how high a price, but it didn't matter. The only price too high to pay was the loss of the city, and its water supply. If it cost him all the gold in the treasury, so be it. The city's wealth was in its water. Without it…the city would die.

"Do it. Find an enchantress powerful enough to save Tasnim from this djinn."

While Philemon waited for the door guardian's return, he sent camel trains to the as yet unnamed oasis, to bring back water for the city. His concubines grumbled at having to surrender their bath to become the household water supply, but Philemon left them no choice. Once a place where water was plentiful, for the first time, Tasnim became like other desert cities, where every drop was precious.

Finally, the door guardian returned. "I have brought your enchantress, Master," the djinn announced. "Allow me to present Lady Zuleika."

She was his height, and she wore her hair uncovered, though it was twisted into a complicated knot on the back of her head, held in place by pins or magic, he wasn't sure. From her proud bearing, she could have been a princess, not just a mere lady.

The door djinn didn't seem to care about introducing him. Philemon sighed. If he wasn't enslaved to Philemon's ring of office, he would have sent the djinn away long ago.

"I am Prince Philemon, a humble prince in need of your help to control a troublesome djinn," Philemon said, bowing deeply.

"What sort of man sends a djinn to find an enchantress to solve his djinn problem?" Lady Zuleika asked. "It seems like a particularly sadistic task to set your poor slave."

Philemon jerked up from his bow and met her amethyst gaze. He'd mistaken her for one of his own people, but her pale eyes and unnatural height marked her as the child of some northern barbarian from the lands where it snowed in winter. He'd heard tales that the northern women fought as warriors alongside their men, much like the women warriors who had once been garrisoned here, and her manners made him believe it. A pity, for the enchantress was young and pretty. She'd make a lovely wife, were her tongue not so waspish.

Those purple eyes blazed. "Look at me like that again and I will leave," she snapped.

Too late Philemon realised his lust had leaked out of his usually controlled expression. Or perhaps this witch had read his mind – he had heard tales of powerful enchantresses who could do such things.

Philemon cleared his throat, trying to clear his mind of thoughts of this girl's body. "This djinn is not the problem. It's the other one. The slave of the lamp. He drained the wells of Tasnim dry and refuses to repair the damage he's done."

Lady Zuleika nodded. "Ah, no wonder the price you offer is so high. Gold is nothing compared to water in the desert. A djinn who makes it disappear must be stopped." She waved a hand. "Show me the djinn who caused the trouble."

Now? It would take his servants some time to make their way to the treasury in the lower levels of the city to retrieve the lamp and bring it back. Time he did not want to spend in the enchantress's company, risking offending her again.

"Summoning the djinn will take time, and you must be tired from your long journey here," Philemon said smoothly. "Allow me to accommodate you in one of the finest guest chambers in the palace. Servants will bring you refreshments, water to wash with, and anything else you need. My other djinn will be your guide in the city, showing you anything you wish to see."

She inclined her head. "Thank you. I have heard great things about the generosity of desert hospitality, but this is the first time I have had the opportunity to experience it for myself."

"You'll have to wait until the water's back before you can use the bathhouse," the door djinn said.

Philemon was struck with the irresistible image of the young enchantress in the harem bathhouse. Desire stirred, and more besides.

"I'll be in my chambers," he called after her and the door djinn. It wasn't a lie. He would be – after a detour to the harem to find a willing concubine or two to sate his desire. Because more than anything, Philemon knew he needed her magic more than he needed another girl in his bed.

Six

Late the next morning, Philemon emerged from his bedchamber, aching in all the right places. Now he could face the enchantress without being distracted.

"Your Highness, Lady Zuleika wishes you to meet her in the lower treasury," a servant said.

Philemon stared. "Before I have broken my fast? The woman is mad. Tell her I shall be with her when I am ready."

The servant bowed and hurried away.

Philemon took his time over breakfast,

knowing he needed to calm his irritation before he faced the enchantress. At least until she had restored their water supply. When he felt he was pleasantly full and he'd regained most of his good mood, he set off for the deepest level of the city.

"Ah, perfect timing," he heard the enchantress say. She beckoned without looking at him. "Philemon, come here and order your djinn to remain in his lamp until his master summons him."

Philemon wasn't sure which was the greater insult – her familiarity, or the fact that she deigned to give him orders.

She made an impatient sound in her throat. "It's the last step of the spell. Once you've said the words, the djinn will not be able to trouble you again. Even if he was ordered by your enemy to destroy the city, as his new master, your orders will take precedence. Hold the lamp in your hands and issue your orders."

Grudgingly, Philemon stepped forward and lifted the lamp in both hands. He cleared his throat. "Slave of the lamp, you are ordered to remain within the confines of your lamp until I summon you." He set the lamp down on a chest by the back wall.

She wrinkled her nose. "Not as precise as I'd like, but it will do. Now, Kaveh told me this is your personal fortune, and not the city's wealth?"

Philemon nodded. "Indeed. The city treasury is on a different level. These rooms hold the gifts personally given to the many generations of princes who have ruled this place."

"So, when you offered half of your personal fortune for an enchantress who can fix your problem here, you meant half of that?"

It hurt to agree – losing so much gold was a blow to any man – but Philemon forced himself to nod. "Half of my fortune for saving the city, yes."

"Good, because I've enchanted all of it. Your half and mine. Anyone who enters this chamber will be filled with such irresistible desire for the gold they see that does not belong to them, that they will not notice the lamp, nor wish to take it from you. Therefore the djinn will remain under your command and inside the lamp, unable to do any further harm to your city." She glanced around. "Perhaps I should ward the door, too, so that no one can open it. Or just you."

Philemon shook his head. "The gold here belongs to the crown – to me, now, but to my successors, should I succeed in siring a son. And princes do not open their own doors. We have servants to do it for us. Here." He rubbed his ring and the door guardian appeared. "If you must enchant the door, make it so that only this djinn can open it. He is the slave to my ring of office, which passes to my son in his turn."

She shrugged, bit her lip, and waved her hand. A faint hint of lavender dust flew through the air and sparkled on the door for a moment before it faded. "There. The djinn will trouble you no more!" She turned her amethyst eyes on him. "Now, I would like to take a small part of my fee with me, but leave the rest here, for this is as safe a place as any." A bag appeared in her hand, sturdy enough to hold a great deal of gold.

So fast? Philemon smiled. "Now you have

returned our water to the city, you have more than earned your fee, Lady Zuleika."

Her eyes grew wide. "Water? Do I look like a water witch? You hired me to deal with a powerful djinn, not fill your water tanks. Which I have now done, so as soon as you pay me for my services, our business will be concluded."

"Unless you restore the water supply to our wells, I will give you nothing!" Philemon shouted. He grabbed the enchantress's arm and dragged her into the corridor. Then he pointed at the door guardian. "Seal the door to the treasury, and do not open it unless your master commands you to do so!"

The round stone door rolled into place behind them.

"Now fix our water, witch!" Philemon said.

Lady Zuleika snatched her arm from his grip and returned his glare. "One you have paid me for the services already rendered, then perhaps I will consider taking a second commission. Until then...I will not help you, and nor will any witch, once they've heard what I have to say."

"I will not pay you a single copper coin until you fix our water supply!"

"And I will do nothing for you until you pay me for what I have already done!"

The door guardian broke the tense silence. "Master, it is unwise – "

"Silence!" Philemon roared. "Remove this woman from the city, and see that she does not return. Then find me a witch who will do as I ask!"

"Then you sentence your city to a slow death by thirst, because of your treachery. No witch will help you now!" Lady Zuleika said.

"What are you waiting for? Seize her, slave!" Philemon snapped.

The door guardian's expression was one of wide-eyed panic, but he could not say a word. He wrapped one arm around the enchantress, pressing his hand to her mouth so that she could not draw the blood she needed to cast a spell. Without magic, her strength was no match for the djinn's as he carried the struggling girl up to the gate.

"Good riddance!" Philemon called after them.

Seven

The sun reminded Anahita of her sister, Maram, the way it wanted to worm its way into her good graces, and Anahita was having none of it. Every bit of her hurt, and the sun would only blind her if she opened her eyes, anyway. Not to mention the gentle warmth she felt now would turn into a raging blaze that seemed to set the very sand on fire. Yet it was as relentless as Maram when she wanted Anahita awake, for she was one who always got her way. No one could resist her for long.

But Anahita would hold out as long as

possible, for they had played this game for as long as she could remember.

An impatient clacking sound got the better of her – Vega did not click her beak lightly.

Finally, Anahita opened her eyes.

Vega flapped her wings, as if to gesture toward her haul. Two fat ducks lay on the sand, and some sort of scurrying creature Anahita could not identify – all dead.

"You've been a busy girl. Which would you like?" Anahita asked, reaching out to stroke the eagle's feathers.

Vega cocked her head to one side, so that one fiery eye could better regard Anahita.

Ah, animals did not understand the nuances of likes and dislikes. Spending so much time among humans without an animal to talk to, she'd forgotten.

"Which is the tastiest?" Anahita asked instead.

Vega did not reply. She closed her beak around the dead scurrier's neck and tugged it closer to herself, opening her wings in a protective mantle over her meal.

"Good choice. Thank you for the ducks,

then. They will break my fast nicely." Anahita reached for them, only to realise there was something else she'd forgotten. Her splinted arm was a pointed reminder about the previous night's events.

"I wondered when you would wake," a male voice said.

Reflex made Anahita reach for a veil to cover her face, but Haidar shook his head.

"No need for that. Asad and I are no longer men. That bastard Fakhri saw to that." He spat on the ground at the mention of the man's name. "May he rot in hell like all the damned for what he did to our village."

"What did he do?" Anahita ventured, though she suspected she knew.

"A few of his men attacked our camp at dusk, luring our warriors out of the village. As the two best warriors, my father left us behind to guard the women and children until they returned. But no one returned, and he had an army hidden in the dunes that descended on us when it was dark. Asad and I are good, but not against so many. He and his men captured everyone who was left, and dragged them back to his camp – even the girl children. He used the little ones first, making us carry out the corpses once he'd finished taking his pleasure of them. I thought he was a demon then, before he started on the women. And my wife…"

"Which one is your wife?" Anahita asked.

Haidar just shook his head and buried his head in his hands.

Asad approached. "Haidar's wife was with child. That bastard tried to cut the child out of her before he took his pleasure of her. She bled to death beneath him in his bed, before he made us carry the corpse out. I'd never been so happy not to marry, but my sisters…ah, we buried them all, until we were the only ones from our village left alive. He was preparing to attack another camp when you arrived and…distracted him." Asad shuddered.

Anahita was silent for a long moment. Finally, she said, "Why did you stay with him? I understand wanting to protect what was left of your people, but if you are all that is left…"

"Because we're slaves. Escaped slaves, now.

Anyone may kill us on sight, or return us to his camp."

She wet her lips. "But…his last order was to guard me, was it not? Take me home to my father, and I will see to it that you are freed. Then you may serve whoever you please, for you will be free men again."

Haidar let out a hollow laugh. "We are no longer men, and we will never be free. My wife and unborn child will haunt me until the day I die."

Asad nudged him. "Anything is better than serving the man who killed them. Where does your father live?"

Anahita smiled faintly. "My father has a grand palace in the capital."

Asad swore, then apologised. "What manner of man sends his daughter to marry a dog like Fakhri?"

"My father has many daughters. I am…the least of them, for my mother was a concubine and not one of his wives. I think he hoped my marriage would bring peace to the desert, to further his trade interests. And perhaps I will, though not the way he thought." Anahita smiled more broadly at that. Playing at politics was the sort of thing Maram did, not a nobody like her.

Haidar fell to his knees on the sand and bowed until his forehead touched the ground. He gestured for Asad to do the same. "Then we will serve you, for we owe you a debt. We swore vengeance on Fakhri, both of us, yet it was you who exacted it. Free or enslaved, we serve you."

Anahita shook her head. "When we reach my father's palace, I will return to the harem, where no men are allowed to enter. You are fighters, warriors, protectors – enlist in my father's guards. He always needs more good men."

Haidar lifted his head. "We are no longer men. Fakhri took from us what you took from him."

It took Anahita a moment to understand what he meant, though he'd said the words before. "You mean he cut off your...?" She couldn't utter the words.

"He made eunuchs of us, yes," Asad supplied. "Guards of his harem. Guarding them against everything except that which would kill them – him."

Anahita didn't know what to say. What did you say to a man who'd had his manhood forcibly removed? Or lost everything he loved, and been forced to serve the man who'd destroyed it?

"Man or not, I vow on my wife's grave that no man will ever hurt you again while I live," Haidar said. He grinned. "My wife would have taken great pleasure in seeing what you did to his corpse."

"And I," Asad added.

"Now all we need to do is get home," Anahita said.

"We will get you there, or die trying," Haidar promised. "What is your name, lady?"

"Anahita," she said slowly, "But in the harem, I was just Ana." She stared down at the rough robes she'd donned to cover herself against the fierce desert sun. She might be a sultan's daughter, but now she was no different to these two men, all fugitives in the desert. "Just Ana," she repeated softly.

Eight

As Philemon returned to his apartments, he found his people staring at him. They'd all heard his argument with the enchantress, then.

"I will address the people of the city at sunset, in the great hall cavern," he said, repeating the words over and over as he ascended the tunnels to his own dwelling.

It wasn't until he reached the privacy of his own chambers that he allowed his stiffened shoulders to slump as despair overwhelmed him. What was he to do now?

Philemon heard the crash of the main gate

slamming open. No one but the djinn door guardian should have been able to do that.

A lesser man would have sent a servant to investigate, but Philemon was the Prince of Tasnim, and he would confront this threat head on.

He rubbed the ring, summoning the djinn guardian. Just because he wasn't a coward, didn't mean he was stupid.

The entry hall was full of dust, turning the people running through it into ghosts and shadows. But ghosts and shadows bent under the weight of whatever it was they carried. Philemon's blood ran cold.

"They can't leave! Don't let them take my treasures!" he shouted.

"As you command, Master," the djinn said, bowing, before disappearing into the gloom.

"Wait. You have to close the door!" Philemon called, but the djinn evidently hadn't heard him, for he didn't return.

"I would only open it again. You can't keep these people here to die," a female voice said. The enchantress.

She strode out of the dust, haloed against

the open doorway like some sort of avenging angel. Philemon shrank away from the fury written across her face.

"You don't deserve this city, or my help, or any magical assistance at all. You demanded my assistance, then lied to me, blaming the dried-up wells on everything but your own stupidity. The djinn of the lamp told me everything. You commanded the djinn of the lamp to destroy your own water supply, not some imaginary enemy. Even after I sent him back into exile, you dared to refuse payment for my services. To evict me from your city. It is your city no longer. Your people flee, for the source of its wealth – the water – is gone, and they cannot live here any more. You deserve this."

Philemon couldn't help himself. "The djinn tricked me! He didn't tell me making that oasis would drain the city wells dry. My princess will never marry me if I am the prince of a city of no people. Make him fix it. Or use your powers to fix it!"

Lady Zuleika shook her head. "I do not take orders from you, Prince of Tasnim. Or should that be prince of a dead, dry cave?"

"Fix it!" he shouted. "You said you would help me!"

"I did help you. And I will do you one further favour. The only way for you to understand what has happened to your city's water supply is to inspect it personally, and you shall!" Purple light erupted from her hands, knocking him back against the wall of the well. But the magic kept pushing at him, leaning him back, until…

Philemon screamed as he fell backward into the well, arms flailing for something to stop him from falling to his death, but the well somehow gaped impossibly wide, and he could not grasp anything.

The fall should have killed him, but it just knocked the wind out of him, so all he could do was lie there on his back in a shallow puddle, listening to the sounds of his people deserting him.

A head appeared above. Hers, of course. "Fix your own plumbing problem. But even then, no woman in her right mind will want a toad like you, prince or not. If you ever find some princess who will take pity on you, take you to her bed and willingly lie in your slimy arms until dawn, maybe I'll find it in my heart to make you human again. For her sake."

And then she was gone.

Philemon reached for his ring of office, to summon the door guardian to lift him out of the well. But his fingers were bare – the ring had somehow fallen off.

He screamed in frustration, a sound that should have echoed around the underground chamber, striking fear in every heart. But the only sound he heard was a forlorn croak.

Nine

Anahita was naked, covered in blood, and Fakhri came for her again, his body glowing red in the light, his jutting cock as long as he was tall. She screamed, and once she started, she couldn't seem to stop.

A hand came from nowhere, pressing down on her mouth so hard she swore there would be a fresh bruise to add to those Fakhri had already given her. She flailed about, trying to fight her way free.

"Hush, Lady Anahita, you are safe. We swore an oath, but we cannot keep it if you scream so loud everyone in the desert hears you."

She knew that voice. Anahita blinked her eyes open to make sure. Yes, it was Haidar. She blew out a breath she hadn't known she'd been holding. "Thank you," she said shakily. "I dreamed…"

Haidar cut her off. "As we all do." He grimaced. "There are some hours to go before nightfall, when we will travel under the cover of darkness again. Try to sleep, for you will need your strength."

She shook her head. "I cannot. Not after such a dream. If his men come after us…"

"They will not. And even if they do, they will not get past Asad and I," Haidar said.

It was on the tip of her tongue to say that Haidar hadn't been able to protect his own wife, the woman he loved, when Fakhri's men had come for her, but she had no desire to remind the man of his loss. Instead, she said, "I got past you. To kill…to kill…" She couldn't even say the sheikh's name, though she had only to closer her eyes to see his evil grin, gleaming above that monstrous cock.

"You were not a threat," Haidar said.

She glared at him. "Enough of a threat to kill him."

"Because he did not see you as a threat, either," Haidar replied. "If you came at me with a knife, you would not kill me so easily." He gazed at her, as though sizing her up for something. "If you truly do not think you can sleep any more, perhaps you should try." He produced a knife from nowhere and offered it to her, hilt first.

Anahita took it. The blade was barely bigger than her eating knife – much smaller than the one she'd killed her husband with.

Haidar backed out of the tent and beckoned for her to join him. "There is more space for a blade dance out here."

It took Anahita longer to join him, between her broken arm and what she suspected were also broken ribs, but no matter how much she hurt, something within her would not let her back down from this fight. She refused to let any man dictate what she could or could not do, ever again.

She stood for a moment, taking in Haidar's

relaxed stance as the afternoon sun set his face aglow. Then she rushed at him, raising the knife above her head.

His arm shot out and slammed against her wrist, sending the blade spinning across the sand.

Her wrist throbbed, already covered in dark bruises from Fakhri, and she cradled it to her chest, fighting back tears. She met Haidar's gaze squarely, refusing to bow her head.

He was the one to look away first, striding across the sand to retrieve his knife. Anahita expected him to tuck it back into its sheath, but he held it out to her instead. When she wrapped her fingers around the hilt, he shook his head. "No, you're holding it wrong. It's easy for someone to knock it out of your hand if you do it like that."

Haidar wrapped a warm hand around hers, showing her how it should be done.

"And don't hold the knife up high like you did just then. He'll see you coming, and have plenty of time to defend himself. Strike from below, like you did the first time. If he doesn't see it coming, he won't block, and your blade will have a better chance of finding its mark. A man rarely looks at what is under his nose, and if you extend the line of his nose down to the ground, you will see where he is blind." He drew a line down his nose and pointed at a spot on the ground. "That is where you lift your blade to do the most damage." He wrapped his hand around Anahita's and brought the blade up to his throat. "Or keep it low, to hit his heart, or his belly." He touched the blade tip to those places on his body, then released her. "Now try it again."

She did, and he corrected her, a sequence they repeated over and over until he was satisfied.

Anahita tried to hand his knife back, but Haidar refused to accept it. Instead, he produced the sheath, and insisted she wear it now she knew how to use it.

"Thank you," she said in wonderment.

"Are you finished with your foolishness now, so that we can be on our way?" Asad asked.

"Teaching her how better to defend herself is not foolishness," Haidar objected.

"She has a broken arm and plenty of other bruises from the bastard's blows. She wouldn't last five minutes in a proper fight." Asad pointed at the fire. "You'd be better off teaching her how to cook. Now that's a more womanly skill."

"She killed a man, with that broken arm, and the other injuries. You couldn't have done it," Haidar said.

Asad shrugged. "I don't have the advantage of being a tiny girl he's beaten into submission more nights than that bastard could count. She surprised him, that's all."

"And us," Haidar said. "You never saw it coming, either, or you wouldn't have let her take your blade. Next time, she may need more than the element of surprise. She's as much a warrior as any of our people were."

"She's not Nasrin," Asad said softly. "Your wife is dead, cousin. Nothing you do now can change that."

Haidar brought up his stubborn chin. "You think I don't know that? That tiny girl avenged Nasrin, and all our people. Her. Not you or me. And she did it after a beating, with a broken arm. That takes courage. You swore to protect her, just as I did. Giving her a blade and training her to use it is part of that oath."

"You're still a fool." Asad turned away to put some more kindling on the fire.

"I'd rather learn to fight than to cook," Anahita said. "I will sleep more soundly for it, even after I am home. Besides, it is Vega and I who do the hunting. It is only fitting that someone else cooks our catch."

Haidar burst out laughing. "The lady is right! A true huntress, and she has trained that bird well."

Anahita considered telling them that she hadn't trained Vega at all, but she wasn't sure how they would react to her ability to speak to animals. Best to keep that a secret a little longer.

"So, shall we practice some more while Asad makes our breakfast?" Anahita ventured with a hopeful smile.

"As my lady commands," Haidar said with a bow. Neither of them paid any attention to Asad's grumbled complaints as he threaded meat onto a knife to cook over the fire.

Ten

When Anahita lifted her gaze to survey the open city gates, she nearly wept for joy. Never had she seen anything so beautiful as that dusty portal. And yet…a princess did not weep before her people, so her tears died the dry death that befell all who did not know the ways of the desert.

"Stop," she commanded, and Asad and Haidar did. More than that, they stared at her in surprise. She summoned the same courage that had driven her to seize the knife that set her free, and said, "This is my father's city. The people must make way for his daughter. One of you must go before me, and the other behind, as befits a princess." She moistened her lips. "All the way to the Sultan's palace. My home."

Haidar coughed, but Asad laughed outright. "Do you truly expect us to believe that? The Sultan would not sacrifice his daughter to an animal like Sheikh Fakhri! Tell us the truth, now, Ana. Which house really belongs to your father?"

If they didn't believe her, who would? "My father is the Sultan, and you will address me as Your Highness Princess Anahita. At least until you are free, and our bargain is fulfilled."

Haidar wouldn't meet her eyes. "And if the guards do not let us into the palace?"

She had not come this far to be denied her home. "Then you will tell them to fetch Princess Maram. My sister will recognise me, and take me to my father."

Haidar grasped her arm. "What will you tell the Sultan?" Panic widened his eyes.

Anahita shook off his hand. "I will tell him the truth. That Sheikh Fakhri is dead at my hand. My father sent me to forge peace with the sheikh, and so I have. He will never attack our people again. Now, please pretend you are my official guards, and make the people make way for their princess."

Haidar grinned. "Never thought I'd get to meet the Sultan. Go on, Asad. You heard the princess. You lead the way, shouting orders to her people. I'll keep watch from the back."

"And if the Sultan has us killed?" Asad hissed, not convinced.

Haidar's grin never wavered. "It is a better death than what we faced in the desert. We should have died with our people. The only reason we're alive now is because Ana stole your knife. She's not afraid of the Sultan. How are you going to live out the rest of your life, knowing you have less courage than that girl?"

Asad glared at his cousin. "If this is a ploy so that you can see Nasrin sooner, I will torment you in the afterlife. I swear it. You will never know a moment's peace." Then he took his place before Anahita and drew in a deep breath. "Make way for the princess!" he bellowed. "Make way for Her Highness

Princess Anahita!"

Anahita straightened her shoulders, wishing she was taller and more impressive, and followed Asad into the city.

The palace gates presented no problem, and they walked straight in. It wasn't until Anahita reached the audience chamber that she realised today must be a public audience day, for the hall was packed.

"Now what?" Asad whispered.

Anahita unfasted the straps that held Vega to her. "Fly home, and see that the falconer gives you a good dinner," she said, lifting her arm high so that the bird might fly. Vega did not hesitate, soaring over the palace to where her meal awaited. If everything went well, Anahita would hunt with her again on the morrow. If not…

"We seek an audience with my father. Make the crowd part," she said, praying they would. The rest of the city had responded as though she was Maram, and not some forgotten concubine's daughter.

A path opened, and Anahita plunged ahead, her men trailing behind her. When she reached the foot of her father's dais, she threw herself down on the floor, blessing the cool marble beneath her forehead. She raised her voice, "Father, I bring news. Sheikh Fakhri is dead."

Silence fell over the hall, stretching for an eternity. Anahita didn't dare look up.

Then she heard the rustle of her father's robes. "Today's audience is at an end. Return tomorrow."

The sounds of a herd of grumbling, shuffling people echoed off the arched ceilings, so only Anahita and those closest to the Sultan heard his words: "Have refreshments bought to my private chambers. I will speak to her there."

Servants helped Anahita to bathe and dress in finer clothes than she'd ever worn before. Long silken sleeves hid her bandaged arm, now wrapped in fresh linen, as gentle hands combed and oiled her hair. It was like being a bride all over again, but there was no fear in her belly this time. Only determination.

When she reached her father's chamber, Anahita prostrated herself again.

"When I announced I was sending one of

my daughters to Fakhri to be his bride, I was advised that I was sending the girl to her death. I was begged to reconsider, for the only language the Sheikh understood was violence. But I kept my word, and you were sent. Now, you return, bringing word of the Sheikh's death. Such a thing is impossible. Therefore, I ask you to explain how it is possible."

"A miracle," Anahita said weakly.

The Sultan sighed. "Get up, girl. I can't hear you when you talk to my rug. Now, tell me everything. Did you marry the man?"

Anahita rose and met her father's eyes. The eyes of the man who had sent her to be beaten to death by Fakhri.

Haidar was right — she'd faced death in Fakhri's eyes, and she had no fear left for her father, the man who'd sentenced her to that fate.

She settled herself on a cushion and poured herself a cup of whatever her father was drinking. She drank half of it down, barely tasting the cold juice, for there was not enough sweetness in the world to dull the bitterness on her tongue.

Anahita took a deep breath, and told her tale.

She left nothing out. Not one blow, or the trials she and her men had endured in the desert. Until, finally, she was done.

Her father opened his mouth to respond.

Perhaps she was not done, after all.

"Sheikh Fakhri deserved his fate, and if you marry me to a pig like that again, I swear I will gut him like the animal he is, too," she said fiercely, then added, almost as an afterthought, "Father."

"Ana!" a female voice shrieked, and a flash of silk and gold flew across the room to embrace Anahita. "You're alive!"

Anahita wanted to warn her sister about her broken arm, but despite Maram's apparent excitement, she had taken great care not to touch Anahita's right arm. Realisation dawned – Maram knew all that had been said and done since Anahita entered the palace, and she'd chosen her time of arrival perfectly.

Maram's tone was one of girlish delight. "Father, you must give her the apartment beside mine. The harem is for virtuous wives, not the likes of us. What reward did you offer the two heroes who carried her home to us?"

If Anahita had not known before, now she was certain Maram's spies had told her everything. For she had not seen Haidar or Asad since the throne room.

She opened her mouth to ask, but both her father and Maram seemed to have forgotten her. No, not Maram, who broke from her chatter to say, "Oh, you must be exhausted! Go and rest – the chambers beside mine, mind, not in the harem. I must discuss my new jewels with Father, but when we are done, I will come to you directly."

Dismissed – by her own sister! – Anahita was too tired to protest. She followed a servant to her new chamber, only to find it larger than the one she and Maram had shared in the harem. But the size didn't matter – all she cared about was the bed, that heavenly soft surface that embraced her as it promised rest.

It seemed but a moment since she'd closed her eyes, but the stiffness of Anahita's limbs told a different story. It was Maram's voice that had woken her – her sister sounding annoyed, which didn't happen often.

"Don't be ridiculous. She is my sister. You wouldn't deny me the chance to be reunited with my dearest sister, who I thought I would never see again?" Maram wheedled.

Haidar sounded chagrined. "No, mistress, I mean, Highness, but our job is to protect Princess Anahita, and unless she says she wants to see you…" A long pause, and Anahita imagined he shrugged. "My deepest apologies."

Anahita staggered to her feet. "Let her in," she said hoarsely, then swallowed and repeated the words.

Haidar stuck his head through the doorway. "Are you sure? I think she's trying to cast some sort of spell. She's bitten her lip bloody. I wouldn't want you to come to harm. First day officially on the job and all, but I'm not that stupid."

Spells. Maram. Seduction spells, surely. Would they work on a eunuch? Anahita was one of the few who knew of Maram's magical talents, for she'd seen her use them often enough.

"Maram, stop. Boys, please let her in. She's

telling the truth. Maram means me no harm," she said.

All three of them entered the room, to Maram's obvious annoyance.

"I will not tolerate the presence of that man's sworn men," Maram said loftily, dismissing them with a wave of her hand. "Begone."

"We are sworn to the Sultan now, more than ever before. The only oath I swore to that whoreson was that he'd die screaming, drowning in his own blood. So when Princess Anahita here delivered the blow that fulfilled my oath, we became her men. Until death." Haidar bowed in Anahita's direction, and Asad did the same.

Only then did Anahita realise they wore guard uniforms, instead of the clothes they'd arrived in. "But you're free…aren't you?" she asked.

Asad laughed. "Free as we ever were. But oaths are tricky things, best not broken. Our village is gone, and we have nowhere else to go. Palace guard seemed like a good idea. Especially if we're to protect the princess outside the harem."

Maram gasped. "They're common desert herders? And your lovers? Are they any good?" Her gazed raked over Asad, then Haidar.

It was Anahita's turn to gasp. "Surely you haven't taken a lover. Not after your mother…"

Maram smiled. "Ah, you haven't heard. Of course I have. While you were off adventuring in the desert, I have been training to become a courtesan. The best the world has ever known. For it will soon be my turn to travel, as Father's ambassador to far-off lands. I would have gone sooner, but Father hesitated, doubting my advice. Now you have returned, he will not doubt me again. I told him Fakhri could only be stopped with weapons. He should have believed me. Sent an army instead of you…" Her hands fluttered in genuine distress. "Is it true that he broke your arm? Where else are you hurt?"

Anahita waved her away. "I'm healing fine. Besides, you don't want to hear about my blisters from walking across the desert. Instead, tell me about your travels. Will you go north to where ice falls from the sky?"

"I hope so." Maram's eyes lit up. "Oh, you would not believe half the things Mistress Kun has taught me. A thousand ways to seduce a man, and a thousand more to enslave him without his knowledge."

Asad hurried out of the room, followed by Haidar.

Maram smothered a laugh. "There. It is good to have you home, Ana. I thought I'd lost you forever. Now will you tell me about your lovers?"

Anahita shook her head. "Asad and Haidar aren't my lovers. They're eunuchs, men Fakhri enslaved from the camps he slaughtered. I've told my tale to Father, and I'm sure you heard all I have to tell. But you have done so much since I left. What of your lovers?"

Maram blushed. "Well…"

Anahita listened, entranced, as Maram spun a tale that seemed like an airy fantasy, of men who could make her body sing, as she learned the arts to bring a man pleasure in equal measure. Yet even as Maram spoke, Anahita fervently wished that such men did exist.

Somewhere.

Eleven

Philemon feverishly searched every inch of the cavern twice over, and still he did not find the ring. He shouted until he was hoarse, but only ominous silence greeted him from above. He feared the city was empty but for him. And the water beneath it was draining away. Even now, the pool that had broken his fall had dried to a couple of shallow puddles.

No matter how high he leaped, he could not catch the lip of any of the wells, which taunted him from above.

But he would not die down here. He was a

prince, by all that was holy.

If he could not return to the city, then he would find another way. The water here had travelled some sort of path between the city and the oasis, and where water went, so could he.

He'd follow the water to the oasis and make his way back to the city across the desert.

He set off along the tunnels, following the sound of flowing water in the darkness. If he faltered, he only had to remind himself that he was not destined for an ignominious end, all alone in the tunnels beneath his city. As long as he lived, so did Tasnim. Step after tentative step, he would reach the oasis.

Hours passed, or perhaps it was days. The darkness was as timeless as the desert above, but it would not defeat him.

When he finally did stop, it was because water barred his way. Not the puddles and shallow stream he'd splashed through, but a pool so deep he could not see the bottom. Yet the water glowed as if lit by some magical underground sun.

No, not an underground one, he realised.

One that burned down from the sky above. He'd found the oasis, but he would have to swim to reach it.

So be it.

The water was cool against his skin, a sweet caress urging him on. He swam for longer than he expected, but not so long that he felt the burn in his lungs from holding his breath too long. When he surfaced into brilliant sunlight, he let out a shout of triumph. No witch would be the end of him!

Was it his imagination, or did the oasis appear bigger than before? Philemon wasn't sure, but the swim seemed to take as long as his walk through the tunnels. But determination drove him, now more than ever before, and he reached the shore.

Desert sand compressed underfoot, gritty and crumbling between his toes. Huh. He must have lost his shoes somewhere in the dark and not noticed until now. Philemon glanced down, but he couldn't see his toes through the dislodged dust swirling through the water. He stepped out.

Pain burned the soles of his feet, like the

fires of hell itself. He bit back a scream and hurled himself back into the water. Slowly, the fire in his feet extinguished in the lapping waters of the oasis.

He would bind his feet with scraps of cloth torn from his robes, the way beggars did, Philemon told himself. Beggars in other cities, for there were none in Tasnim.

He reached for the hem of his robe, but he clutched only air. Now he looked down again, really looked, and this time he couldn't tear his eyes away. No amount of water could hide the green tint to his skin, or the peculiar shape of his feet.

Philemon held his hands up to his face, praying that they would be normal, but his prayers were not answered. His green hands had only four fingers each.

A toad, the witch had called him, not a prince.

She'd turned him into one.

He let out a scream of fury, but all that came out was a croak.

Swearing he'd hunt down the witch and force her to fix the mess she'd made, he sank beneath the surface. Watching. Waiting. For frogs could not survive in the desert alone – he would need to find a travelling party to join to take him back to Tasnim. Or, better yet, to where he could find the witch.

A caravan would come, he told himself with confidence. And when it did, he would be ready.

Twelve

"I have not left the palace for weeks, and now Vega's found herself a mate, she's not leaving the nest any time soon. I want to go hunting, and to hunt I need a new bird. A hawk this time, smaller than Vega, and not so heavy." Anahita looked from Haidar to Asad. "I saw a new caravan come into the city last night. A new caravan means new birds, or at least I hope so, and who knows what else. Who's coming?"

Asad and Haidar exchanged a glance. "As long as we don't end up spending hours at the goldsmith again," Asad began.

"We weren't there for hours. And it would have been a much shorter visit if you hadn't been fondling that new blade of yours and scaring the man," Anahita said.

"I was testing the edge!" Haidar protested.

"Mm. Testing the edge while wagering how many blows it would take to cut a man's hands off." Anahita set her hands on her hips. "I still don't believe you could do that in one stroke. All that bone…it would take at least two."

"It only took one to deal with that thief who tried to take your purse last time," Asad said.

Anahita waved his words away. "That was you, with your sword. Not Haidar with a knife. And you took off half his arm, not just his hand. Please don't do that again."

Asad looked aghast. "You'd prefer to let thieves steal from you? Your father would assign you a squad of guards, convinced we are not capable of protecting you."

"I'd prefer not to have a screaming man lying at my feet, bleeding all over the place, while the marketplace erupts into chaos and closes before I have finished my shopping,"

Anahita said drily.

"You shall have it. Now no one dares get close enough to us to risk losing their arm, too," Asad said.

Anahita nodded. She had to admit, he had a point. Better that they had a reputation for being fearsome than having to deal with a squad of her father's guards, like Maram did, or being forced to defend herself. If a princess hacked off someone's hand in the marketplace, Father would never marry another daughter off again. Though that might not be a bad thing…

Anahita mentally shook herself. Just because she only knew the undesirable kind of husbands, did not mean her sisters could not be happily married to good men. Fakhri had been the worst, but her other three husbands had not been much of an improvement. Well, unless you counted the fact that all three had not had the opportunity to enjoy married life for very long, and she'd been widowed without any broken bones or significant bruises. True to his word, Haidar had taught her well. So well that she was never without a blade or three within reach.

"Have you changed your mind?" Haidar asked.

He read her expression well. As he should, after so many years together.

"No. Just…a widow's memories are not always pleasant," she said.

Asad laughed. Inside her palace apartments, he knew better than to speak freely, for every wall had ears. He would have to wait until they went hunting to say what was on his mind. And he would, she was certain. For though they kept up the façade of mistress and her sworn men, they were her friends more than anything. The only two truly good men she'd ever met, eunuchs or not.

Maram laughed at her cynicism, as well she might, for Maram charmed men as easily as breathing. But Maram was off travelling again, on some diplomatic mission for her father. Furthering trade somewhere in the far north, where ice lay on the ground for half the year. Anahita shivered at the very thought of it. She was a desert princess, only comfortable when the heat rising up from the sands was warmer than her blood. And boats? Ugh. Give her a camel any day, a creature she could communicate with that would do whatever she said.

But today was for birds, not camels.

"So, are you coming?" she asked.

Despite their initial grumbling, once they were in the bazaar, both men spent more time looking at the wares for sale than she did. Strange foreign blades, cloth so heavy it was a wonder anyone could walk while wearing it…these must have come by ship from the northern lands.

She prayed they'd brought some new creatures. If not a bird, then perhaps something else. One of the wives in the harem had a particularly fat cat that slept on her bed at night, for she abhorred mice and would go nowhere without the beast. Anahita had often wondered whether her father tolerated the animal on the nights he favoured that wife, but she'd never been brave enough to ask.

Maram would know. She knew every secret in the harem. Perhaps the ships had brought her home, too…

But there was no word of Maram's return in the marketplace, as there certainly would be, for she was well known. Instead, the people talked of a sheikh raiding their borders, enslaving those he did not kill. His men had run afoul of a party of crusaders, but the northerners were weak from hunger and war, and the sheikh's men had taken everything from them before leaving them in the desert to die. No one liked the crusaders much, but it was the height of dishonour to let them die in the desert instead of killing them outright. And the stories about this new sheikh made him sound like a second Fakhri.

An affronted shriek drew Anahita's attention from the marketplace gossip. An avian shriek, she was certain, though it didn't sound like a bird she knew. Anahita quickened her pace.

She reached the menagerie, only to discover she'd somehow left Asad and Haidar behind. She debated whether to retrace her steps or simply wait for them to appear.

"What are you looking for today, mistress?" the stall owner asked, offering her a deep bow.

Veiled and shrouded in widow's garb, Anahita didn't bother to correct him. "A hunting bird," she said.

The man's eyes widened. "A song bird might amuse you more, mistress. I have here a bird from the far north with a song so sweet, it will bring tears to your eyes."

"Her Highness has shed too many tears of grief. She delights in hunting, and wishes for your best hawk," Haidar said, appearing at Anahita's elbow.

The man threw himself down on the ground, wailing his apologies and other boring things. Anahita's attention was caught by a prickly ball that suddenly moved. It unrolled, revealing a downy belly and pointed face.

"What is that?" she asked, pointing.

The man clambered to his feet and puffed out his chest. "It is a most rare creature, found only in – "

"It's a desert hedgehog," Asad said flatly. "You'll find a dozen of them at any oasis. I'll catch you one next time you go hunting, Your Highness."

The man deflated. "I assure you – "

He was drowned out by a shriek just like the one that had drawn Anahita's attention in the first place.

This time, she could see the source. And what a source.

The hawk was small, her chest patterned in an intricate mosaic of brown, gold and white. She opened her silvery beak to shriek again, flicking her talon at something pink on the floor of her cage. A baby mouse or rat, Anahita decided.

"Are dead mice not good enough for you, beautiful?" she asked the bird.

"He has given me nothing suitable to eat for many days. I am hungry and this is not food!" the little falcon said. "I must be free to fly and hunt!"

"That is a crusader falcon, from the north," the salesman said smoothly.

Asad shrugged. "I've never seen a bird like it. Have you?"

Haidar shook his head.

"She belonged to a foreign king, who gave the bird as a gift to his mistress, who could not bear to look upon the creature after he died valiantly in battle," the salesman continued. "She was taken prisoner by a vicious sheikh, the same man who killed her paramour, and the bird is pining for his mistress. He needs a new mistress, as royal as the first…"

"My master sold me to pay his passage on a ship home," the bird said. "He knew good food. Fresh food, from the hunt!"

For once, Anahita was glad of her veil, for it hid her smile. "The bird looks thin and hungry. But it's not eating. Is it sick?"

The man began to sweat. "If Her Highness wishes for a more robust bird, may I suggest – "

"How much for the sick bird?"

"For Her Highness, I recommend – "

Haidar named a price that was far too low for the sweet little falcon.

Five minutes later, they left the stall, with Asad carrying the falcon's cage.

Not jewels or silks or the costliest carpet could catch Anahita's eye after that. She made one more stop, at a stall selling snacks and drinks, before demanding that Haidar and Asad accompany her out of the city.

She'd made sure to buy a selection of their favourite cakes, so neither man complained as they took her to one of her favourite hunting spots.

Thirteen

Darkness had descended by the time Anahita headed back inside the city gates. The guards called a challenge, but the moment they spotted Haidar and Asad, they moved aside, bowing to let them pass.

Anahita cradled her new bird to her chest, stroking her feathers as the falcon slept off her fresh-caught feast. Anahita had never seen a bird fish before, but this one seemed born to it, plucking fish and frogs out of the oasis faster than she'd seen her little brothers gobble treats. The bird had laid the first corpses at her feet, and Anahita had thanked her, before telling her she could eat her fill today without needing to share.

As they passed through the bazaar, now lit by torches and busier than ever, there was a buzz that had nothing to do with some sheikh or rumours of distant battles. No, this was the buzz of energy that only came when Maram arrived home. Some claimed they had seen her, while others swore they would line the streets on the morrow, hoping to catch a glimpse of her on her way to the public bathhouse that would be closed for her private use.

Anahita had no idea why her sister chose to patronise the ancient public bathhouse instead of the perfectly private one in the palace, but the people loved that she did.

Anahita had her own reasons to be happy Maram was home. She would have stories to tell about her travels, gifts she'd been given by the people of the various courts she'd visited, and as the Sultan's favourite daughter, her apartments were as opulent as a queen's. So when Anahita joined her for dinner this evening – as she always did when Maram was home – it would be a far pleasanter affair than eating alone, for Haidar and Asad weren't supposed to share her meals. And of course, Maram had charmed the palace cooks like she did everyone else, so the delicacies at her table outshone even the Sultan's feasts. Not to mention the exotic things she brought home from her travels.

The next morning found her fuzzy-headed from the strong berry wine Maram had generously plied her with, but the fuzziness faded fast when Haidar opened the door to her chamber.

"A message from the Sultan, Your Highness," he said gravely.

The message was important enough to be delivered by one of the Sultan's wives. Anahita's heart sank. She was usually beneath the notice of the wives, except when a marriage was in the wind. Then, the highest ranking wife delivered the order. Unwillingly, Anahita sank to her knees. "Your Majesty," she murmured. It was a safer bet than remembering the woman's name.

The wife flashed her teeth in a mirthless

smile. "Princess, you are commanded to travel to the camp of Sheikh Basit, where you will become his bride. You will depart in a week."

Anahita grimaced. While she didn't know this woman's name, Basit was the name that had been on everyone's lips in the marketplace yesterday.

Her father intended to send her to her death again. Would he ever learn? Or perhaps he liked things this way.

Anahita mumbled something about how grateful she was to the wife and the Sultan for making this match for her. Whatever she said, it met with the wife's satisfaction, and she left.

The door clicked shut, and only then did Anahita let rip with the most colourful swear words she could come up with at this latest development.

"Another marriage?"

She looked up. Asad had managed to enter the room on hunter's feet, silent as ever.

"To Sheikh Basit."

He nodded. "Another bastard, no doubt. The marketplace was abuzz about him. When do we leave?"

Anahita didn't hesitate. "Five days. Before Father's official party is prepared, so it's just the three of us. Can you tell Haidar?"

Asad bowed, grinning. "Of course. He'll be as happy to get out of the palace as I am. Are you bringing your new bird?"

Anahita felt a pang of regret, not taking Vega with her for the first time. But Merlin, the frog-hunting falcon, would be a suitable companion for the journey. "Of course I'm taking my bird. Someone has to take her hunting. Think of all the oases on the way."

"I hope Princess Maram brought home some barbarian recipes for cooking frogs, then," Asad called back as he left.

Ugh. Merlin could keep her frogs. Anahita wasn't letting one near her lips, cooked or otherwise.

Fourteen

"This is new. See, the colour of the water? It has not lain here long. And there are no trees yet, though those will grow." Asad nodded at a clump of tiny date palms. "We will camp here for the night," he said, and neither Haidar or Anahita argued.

Anahita eyed the sparkling water, clearer than the other, muddy oases they'd seen along the way. She longed to bathe, after so many days collecting dust as they traversed the desert, and this oasis looked too tempting to resist.

Haidar seemed to have read her mind. "You bathe while we set up camp. Then that bird of yours can hunt while we start a fire to cook whatever it catches."

"Don't let her cook it, or she'll poison us all," Asad said.

They all laughed. None of them would ever forget Asad's failed attempts to teach her to cook. Anahita could manage two cooking styles – charred or raw, neither of which was particularly edible.

"I wager that bird of yours won't catch much. The oasis is too new for anything to live in it yet. Perhaps in a few seasons you will have better luck. Good thing I have plenty of dried meat to season the stew," Asad continued.

"I'll take that wager," Haidar said smoothly. "Desert creatures find water faster than you give them credit for. And that bird has sharper eyes than your dull ones."

Anahita left the boys to bicker while she went to bathe. She stripped off her clothes, folding them beside the water's edge, and stepped into the water's embrace. It was colder than she'd expected, especially after being warmed all day by the sun. For all that it was a new oasis, the waters must run deep to stay so cool.

She immersed herself fully, gasping as it felt like cold fingers reaching for her, stroking away the dust and sweat of the journey as she plunged in deeper.

"Your bird's getting jealous!" Asad shouted.

Reluctantly, Anahita set her feet on the lakebed and turned to see what the fuss was about.

"Frog! Frog!" Merlin screeched, flapping her wings.

"Set her free," Anahita commanded, striding out of the water. She looked at her discarded clothes for a moment, before deciding she wanted fresh things. She rummaged through her bags, seeking something practical among the finery. By the time she'd dug out a suitable tunic, the warm desert wind had dried her skin, so it was a simple matter to slip the garment over her head.

When she turned around, she found Haidar's eyes fixed on her, though he had a faraway look on his face.

"What is it?" she asked softly, keeping her voice low so that Asad would not hear.

Haidar shook his head, and seemed to see her again. "Forgive me, but you reminded me of…happier times."

Times spent with his wife, Nasrin, she knew. "If I could return her to your arms, and make you whole again, I would. You know that."

Haidar sighed deeply. "I know. As would I. But sometimes I wonder if I am a fool for not —"

An unearthly shriek split the air as Merlin erupted from the oasis, beating her wings frantically. She flew erratically, lurching from one side to another, as though she'd drunk too much wine.

"Merlin, come here!" she called. The bird moved toward her, still flying clumsily, and Anahita kept talking, reassuring the bird until Merlin flopped in a heap at Anahita's feet.

Forgetting everything but the bird before her, Anahita knelt down. There was something strange stuck to the bird's face. She reached out to free Merlin.

Fifteen

Something warm gently tugged at his hand, unfastening it from his death grip around the bird's neck feathers. He struggled to keep his legs wrapped around that deadly beak, but that slid out of his grasp, too, as he was surrounded by something warm and soft. It almost reminded him of that night two of his concubines had agreed to share him, and his bed had become a paradise of perfumed, female flesh…

The annoyed chittering of a bird – the same one who'd tried to eat him? – dragged

Philemon out of his delightful daydream. His harem was no more. He sighed.

"You're a strange one, aren't you?" a female voice purred. "I've never heard a frog sigh before. And Merlin tells me they don't usually scream until her master cuts their legs off."

"Then Merlin is a barbarian," Philemon declared.

She sounded amused. "Merlin is a bird. The bird whose face you sat on while you were screaming. Apparently her prey is usually more resigned to their fate. And less inclined to call her names. What sort of frog are you?"

Philemon blew out an exasperated breath and dared to open his eyes, only to find another pair, inches from his own. They were the colour of a desert oasis, wavering between blue and green like water reflecting the sky and the fringing palm trees. But perfectly calm and still, as though it didn't bother her in the slightest that she held a frog in her cupped hands — both hands, for they were not large — as she conversed with him.

The bird's barbarian mistress, Philemon decided, for she wore no veil over her dark hair, and her face was bare for all to see.

"I am not a frog at all, but a prince, under a terrible curse," he announced.

The girl chuckled, a deeper sound than he'd expected from such a small woman. "And did the curse also turn your vast kingdom into that tiny oasis? Are your people swimming about as fish in that water?"

Philemon cast her a scornful glance. "Of course not. That's a story for children, which my mother told me when I was a boy. I am Prince Philemon of Tasnim, a ruler in my own right, and one of the richest men in the region, if not the world." When she seemed unable to reply (too humbled by his high stature, he supposed), Philemon graciously added, "You may address me as Your Highness."

Those blue-green eyes danced. "I don't think I will, Philemon the frog. But my sisters call me Anahita, or simply Ana, and you may, too."

Definitely a barbarian, who had no respect for rank. Philemon sniffed. "You must take me to find the cruel enchantress who cast this terrible curse. When she sees the error of her ways and lifts the curse, you will see me in my true glory, and apologise for your disrespect, for which I will forgive you."

She nodded gravely. "A kind offer, I'm sure, but one I won't accept. I have a wedding to attend, Philemon, and unless your enchantress intends to be one of the wedding guests, you won't find her with me. I will just have to live without your forgiveness." She set him down on the sand and started to walk away.

"Wait!" The word was out of his mouth before Philemon could stop it. She was the first person he'd seen since leaving Tasnim – no one came to this oasis, and if she didn't help him, he might be stuck here for the rest of his life. How long did frogs live for, anyway? Not long, with birds like that monster Merlin around. "You must help me."

She stopped. "Why, Philemon the frog? Why must I help you?"

He hopped across the burning sand, hissing, before he reached the hem of her robe. He hesitated for only a moment before hopping onto the toe of her shoe. The relief was immediate – no more burning sand under his backside. "Because I'll die out here if you don't. I cannot leave the oasis, for I would not last long on the desert sands." He swallowed, forcing the words out. "Please take me with you."

She cupped him in her hands, lifting him so that they saw eye to eye once more.

"So you have some courtesy, after all. If you wish me to carry you across the desert, you must pay for your passage, Philemon the frog. What can you offer that might be of value to me?"

"A chest of gold from the treasury in Tasnim," he answered instantly. "Enough gold to last you a lifetime."

The girl shook her head. "There is no gold here, Philemon the frog. This is not Tasnim, and I will not take you there. For an empty promise, I will take you nowhere."

He opened his mouth to protest that it was not an empty promise at all, before he remembered that he might never make it to Tasnim without her help. He swallowed. "Very well. I will be an amusing travel companion, to make your journey easier and more comfortable, and when I reach Tasnim, I will see that you get your gold." Her hands around him felt like pure bliss compared to the baking desert. "If you carry me with you to wherever you are going, I will give you whatever is in my power to grant you."

She gave a low whistle. "Gold, a helpful travel companion, and a boon. You offer a great deal for someone so small. It seems almost too good to be true." She turned. "What do you think, Merlin?"

Philemon glimpsed the bird, a fiery-eyed hawk, on the ground behind him and flattened himself against Anahita's hands so that the bird wouldn't see him.

The bird let out a shrill chirp.

Anahita laughed. "Merlin thinks frogs are only good for eating. Her previous master was fond of the legs, grilled over a fire, and he gave her the rest."

Philemon shivered. What sort of barbarian ate frogs?

"But I prefer duck," Anahita continued, "and while I already have all the travel companions I need, one who has new tales to tell would be a welcome distraction. Do you know any amusing tales, Philemon the frog?"

He had to think about that one. "My concubines often complimented me on my wit, the quality of my conversation, and the cleverness of my tales," he said finally. They'd also complimented him on his prowess in the bedchamber, but he didn't think this girl was looking for a lover.

Her oasis eyes turned cold. "Concubines. My, you must have been a mighty prince indeed, ruling over such a harem. I cannot imagine why an enchantress would choose to curse you."

"Nor I," he said softly, daring to hope.

She sighed. "Fine, I shall help you. But if you prove to be a nuisance, I will feed you to Merlin."

He swallowed, knowing he would regret this. "Then we have an accord."

Sixteen

"Philemon, I have a proposition for you," the girl called. What had her name been? Oh, that's right – Anahita. No title, no family name, just…Anahita. He should remember that, in case he ever caught himself thinking about her bathing naked in his oasis again. It had been a long time since he'd seen a woman, let alone a naked one, and her form was pleasing enough to catch the eye of a man starved for female company.

Not her face, though. Now he'd seen it up close, he thought her plainer than ever. Her nose was crooked, as though it had been broken. Perhaps barbarian girls fought like boys did. And those strange eyes…like one of the crusaders from the north. She was probably the spawn of some crusader and a girl he stole from her family. That she lived meant her mother had lived long enough afterwards to bear the child – probably as a common whore.

How low he had fallen. A prince, deigning to listen to a proposition from some whore's bastard daughter.

Philemon lifted his head from the water, just enough so that she could see his eyes. "Do you now?"

She smiled. It improved her looks, at least a little.

"You did say you would make my journey more comfortable, did you not?"

Philemon let out a noise that sounded alarmingly like a croak.

She appeared to take this as assent. "You may start by making yourself useful tonight. This lovely oasis of yours is home to a great number of mosquitoes, which have taken up residence in my tent. Given your natural talents with flying things, you shall sit at the end of my bed and keep them from bothering me as I sleep."

It was an order, not a request, and as such, it rankled. But they did have a deal, and, besides, he had to admit he was hungry. He'd give a whole bag of gold for a well-spiced roast lamb, but his accursed body demanded a different form of sustenance.

He raised his head higher, lifting his chin in what he hoped looked like lofty condescension. "Carry me to your bedchamber, and I shall protect you in a true princely fashion."

She burst out laughing.

Philemon glared. "What is so funny?"

She took her time getting control of herself before she finally said, "You really shouldn't do that. It only draws attention to that bulging thing under your chin. On a man, it would be a prominent Adam's apple, but on a frog, it's…a vocal sac of some sort. Terribly distracting, especially when you're talking. I'm too worried it will pop like a soap bubble to listen to a word you say."

Philemon tucked his chin down firmly. "I said carry me to your bed, and I shall protect you in a true princely fashion."

She still smiled, but at least she didn't laugh. "Well, you should know you'll be the first prince to ever protect me in any fashion." She scooped him up and carried him toward her tent.

Philemon had to force himself to hold his tongue. Of course she'd never been protected by a prince before. She'd probably never even met one. But barbarian or not, he had a deal with this girl, and he would honour it, for a prince's honour was a weighty thing indeed.

"I will need a bucket of water, if you wish me to stay in your tent all night. I cannot be allowed to dry out, so I must immerse myself periodically," he said as the tent flaps closed behind her.

She set him on the floor, which was a surprisingly fine carpet. Her bed was equally surprising — as big as his own, when he'd travelled, with several cushions that looked to be made of silk. Stolen, he was certain.

"I'll go fetch some," she said, heading back out the way she'd come.

The moment she was out of sight, he leaped across the carpet for the pallet, aiming for the nearest silk cushion. Oh, how he'd missed the feel of silk against his skin. The only fabric that felt like a woman's caress, which he'd missed for even longer.

But the moment his feet touched the cushion, he experienced nothing so sensuous. No, what he felt next could only be described as every bit of his body sneezing at exactly the same time.

Seventeen

A normal princess would have brought a maid, and a whole troop of servants to see to her needs, Anahita reflected as she dug through their things for a bucket. A normal princess wouldn't have to find her own bucket, and use it to fetch water for an unusually arrogant frog.

But Anahita had never been, and would never be, a normal princess. None of her father's other children had her gift of being able to converse with creatures. In fact, aside from herself and Maram, none of the others seemed to have any magical abilities at all.

Which was why Maram was destined to be alone, and if it weren't for Haidar and Asad, Anahita would be, too. But the three of them made perfect travel companions, because they knew each other so well, and she would trade a whole palace full of servants to take these two men with her.

Servants would only complicate matters. So, with a sigh, she carried her bucket to the oasis and lugged the slopping load to her tent. For the haughty frog.

She shouldn't have agreed to let him come with them. She didn't need another pet – and this one might prove to be a dangerous distraction. Even bringing Merlin with her risked losing the bird, after the way Fakhri had claimed Vega for his own, all those years ago. What if this new sheikh was just as bad, trying to take everything from her so she would be an obedient wife?

Two words that should never be used to describe her: obedient, or wife.

As Fakhri had found out, in his final moments.

His lifeblood flowed over her hands again,

warm and sticky as the night it happened. For she would never forget. Even her arm ached at the memory.

But it was a memory – no more. No man would ever share her bed again.

Anahita took a deep breath, and another, attempting to calm herself. So that she would not appear agitated in front of a frog. She choked back a laugh. Frogs could not discern facial expressions.

She ducked through the tent flaps, stepped inside, then straightened. And stopped dead.

The bucket slipped from her suddenly nerveless fingers, splashing water up to the very roof of the tent, and soaking her to the skin, but Anahita did not feel it.

A rich, mellow voice called out, "Why, you are quite the loveliest woman I have ever seen, under those shapeless things!"

Anahita closed her eyes, but she couldn't seem to shut out his voice, which made things curl up in her belly. So she opened her eyes again, and took in the scene, as Asad had taught her to do.

A lean, muscled man, his skin gleaming in

the lamplight, reclined on her cushions, his dark eyes gazing on her with obvious approval. Other parts of his anatomy rose to salute her, too. Bits she'd hacked off and burned in a brazier…

Anahita turned on her heel and marched out of the tent.

Asad and Haidar rose from their seats by the fire.

"What's wrong?' Haidar asked. "I've never seen you look so pale."

Asad squinted at her. "Me neither. Not since that first night, when – " Haidar waved him into silence, but it was too late.

The night Fakhri died was uppermost in her mind, as it was in theirs.

Anahita fought to keep her breathing even. "There is a man in my bed. An amorous one." She couldn't suppress a shudder.

"There can't be," Asad scoffed. "We've been sitting here all night. No one could have gotten past us and into your tent without us seeing him. You must have imagined him."

It wouldn't be the first time she'd imagined such a thing, and they all knew it. Her memories sometimes rose up so strong, it would take all three of them to banish them back to the past, where they belonged. But she hadn't known this man — all he'd had in common with her long-dead husband was his mighty erection, and his unwelcome presence in her bed.

Anahita lifted a shaky finger and pointed at the tent. "Then you go in there. And tell me what you see, for I will not sleep in that tent unless I know my bed is empty."

Haidar led the way. "Real or imaginary, I will remove him. Asad will help, as he's so certain no one could have gotten past him."

Anahita folded her arms across her chest and stood by the fire, watching the men enter the tent.

The brazier silhouetted them against the tent wall as they leaned down, then came up with a third man between them.

A sob escaped from her lips, before she got hold of herself.

Then she blinked, and three men became two. The mystery man had vanished.

"How dare you!" a thin, reedy voice

screeched. "The girl herself invited me into her bed! For laying hands on me, I shall have you executed!"

Faster than any frog should, the creature leaped across the sand and back into the oasis with an audible plop, still grumbling about faithless women, jealous men and methods of execution.

Haidar emerged from the tent, looking disgruntled. "He was here, and we lifted him off your bed, but then it felt like he slipped through my fingers, and now he is gone. Almost as though we all imagined him." Haidar held out his hand. "But my hand is wet – look!" Moisture shone in the firelight.

"The cushions have wet spots, too, look." Asad stuck his head out of the tent flaps and held out a cushion.

"I spilled a bucket of water. It probably splashed on them," she said, but not even she believed her own words.

Instead, she turned over Philemon's words in her mind. A cursed prince. He might not be a prince, but there was something magical about him. Magic that had made him into a man, if only for a moment.

And on the morrow, she would insist he tell her the whole story of how it happened. That would make the unwanted journey go faster.

"Well, if he's gone, I'm going to bed," she said, and the two men moved aside to allow her entry. Sleep came surprisingly swiftly to her that night.

Eighteen

Philemon sat in the water for a long time, seething. How dare those barbarian boys lay hands on him – a prince? If it had been the girl, he might have forgiven her – she was pretty enough to suit his tastes, and for that one glorious moment, he'd been human again. Desire had flared in her eyes for that moment, too. He hadn't imagined it.

But those men had ruined everything when they seized him and he'd turned back into a frog. He'd watched them from the water, and he was certain neither was her husband. She moved too freely for a wed woman. The easy familiarity between all three of them was the sort he'd known among the city guards before his father had died and he'd claimed the crown. Like brothers. They could be her brothers, though she was tiny compared to them. The child of a second wife, perhaps.

When all three of them retired to the same tent, he was certain of it. Two older brothers, protecting their younger sister. An untamed girl who was more than old enough to wed, but had not yet been taught the proper decorum for a married woman. Her husband would see to that, he was sure of it. The men of the desert demanded much of their wives.

He'd had concubines like her. Girls their fathers could not find suitable marriages for, so they'd been given to him as part of the price for the hospitality of Tasnim. Girls who had taken to Tasnim like ducks did to water, for Tasnim was different to other desert cities.

A city he had to save at any cost, or he had no right to call himself its prince.

He could wait in the oasis for a proper caravan, but who knew how long that would take? These three were the first travellers he'd seen since he took up residence here, and he had delayed long enough already.

He'd struck a bargain with the girl, wild though she was, and something told him she would honour it. But just in case she changed her mind, he would find a place among their things to stow away. The half-filled water bucket outside her tent seemed the most sensible place, he decided, when the night air had cooled the sands enough for him to hop across the camp to investigate.

He settled in the bucket to doze until dawn.

Nineteen

Avian shrieks and swearing woke Anahita from a sound sleep. She did some swearing of her own as she stuck her head out of the tent into the pre-dawn light, where Merlin appeared to be fighting with the water bucket.

"Surrender, foul foe, or I shall drown you!" came the reedy voice of Philemon.

Merlin's head appeared to be stuck in the bucket. She flapped her wings, lifting herself and the bucket a short distance off the ground, before dropping again.

"I do not jest, minion of hell!"

Anahita strode over to rescue them both. She stuck her hand in the bucket and pulled out the frog, who had his tiny arms around Merlin's head. Again. Sighing, she pried them loose. Merlin flapped away with an indignant squawk, shaking off water.

Anahita lifted the frog up so she could look him in the eye. "You're a troublemaker, aren't you?"

The frog puffed up in indignation. "I am a troublemaker? What about that dishonourable demon of a bird, attacking a man in his sleep, no less! I was merely defending myself! Why, if I but had my sword…"

"You have a frog-sized sword? I'd like to see that," Anahita interrupted.

Could a frog glare? She suspected that's what he was doing.

"A sword fit for a prince, from before I was cursed," he said stiffly. "Of course."

"Of course," she repeated. "Are you sure you want to ride with us, seeing as I travel with Merlin?"

He drew himself up. "I am on a quest to save my city from the witch who cursed me. If you had a hundred such birds, I would still fight every one of them in order to succeed at my quest. I am a prince!"

"So you keep saying," Anahita said.

"You saw my princely magnificence with your own eyes last night. How can you doubt me?"

She burst out laughing. "Princely magnificence? Is that what you call a naked man where you're from? I'm not sure what I saw last night. You're no normal frog, but whether you are truly a frog or a man, I do not know." She thought for a moment, then added, "But no matter what you are, I am certain you will prove an amusing travel companion. You may ride with me today, and tell me all about your quest and the city you wish to save."

The frog executed a bow, or at least he tried to. "It would be my pleasure."

Twenty

Anahita refused to allow Philemon to ride in a bucket on the back of her camel, where he would be a terrible temptation for her bird, or so she said, so she and Philemon reached a compromise. He rode in the neck of a half-filled water bag that was strapped in front of her saddle.

"I feel like a wax stopper," he complained.

Veiled against the sand, still she brought her hand to cover her mouth as she giggled. "Most stoppers don't have eyes. Nor are they small enough to slip inside the water bag if Merlin decides she wants to attack you again."

He glanced around, but he could not see the murderous bird. "Where is the creature?"

"She's riding with Asad on the lead camel. Leaving me free to listen to your tales while we travel. So, tell me about your quest, Philemon the frog."

There was little to tell yet, for it had just started. "Have you ever been to Tasnim?" he asked.

She shook her head, sending ripples through the white fabric of her veil. It was too big for her — more suited to one of the men she travelled with than a delicate young woman. No wonder she took it off in camp. "This would have been my first time, but the gates were closed to us."

Her first journey away from her people, Philemon guessed. Then he registered the rest of her words — the gates of the city were closed. He breathed a sigh of relief. No one would loot the place in his absence. Good.

"Until the oasis where you found me formed, Tasnim was the only water source for miles in any direction. An underground citadel in the desert, impregnable and impossible to besiege." He smiled. He was right to be proud of his city. "No one knows who built the first tunnels, but it was used in times of war and the ancients kept a permanent garrison there. Some of the city's present day residents are descended from those soldiers." Even him, for the city's princes had sometimes taken brides from the city people instead of looking further afield, as Philemon had.

"We saw no sign of soldiers. No sign of anyone, actually, no matter how loudly Haidar knocked at the door."

A barbarian girl and her brothers could not afford Tasnim's hospitality, though it was likely there had been no one left in the city to offer it this time.

"They must have fled the curse," Philemon said. "But had they not, they still might not have opened the gates. The price for Tasnim's hospitality is high. Why, I have known men who have sold their daughters to pay the price."

Her eyes – the only part of her face he could see – narrowed. "Perhaps that is why the witch cursed you and your city. Hospitality is one of the sacred laws of the desert."

She was painfully close to the truth, and yet so far from it, too. "We offered her our hospitality, including apartments in my own palace, for a price that should have been a trifle for someone with magic. Yet she refused to cast the spell. She tried to hold us to ransom."

"Did she turn everyone into frogs? Or just you?"

Anahita was observant. Too observant. "Just me. My people…she let them leave, unharmed."

"So you offended the witch somehow. You must have been particularly rude for her to transform you. I've only heard of a few enchantresses who are capable of such complicated magic, and they would need a really good reason to do it. What did you do, Philemon the frog?"

"Why must I be guilty? Perhaps the enchantress envied me the wealth of Tasnim, and wished to take the city for herself!" Philemon said.

Those narrowed eyes did not believe a word of it. "Perhaps. What sort of wealth did Tasnim have? It just looked like a pile of rocks in the desert to me."

"Have you seen the Sultan's palace in the capital?" Philemon didn't wait for her answer. "Tasnim outshines it tenfold. Maybe more. Even the common people's houses have costly mosaics on the walls. In my own palace, no wall or ceiling is unadorned. Every ruler throughout history has commissioned artwork to commemorate their reign, some of which are in the palace, but many are in the city itself. Why, my great grandmother, the Regent Princess Khurshid, had the ceilings of all the public meeting chambers painted to resemble the sky at different times of day. Dusk and dawn, midnight, noon…ah, the work is exquisite. Even now, gazing up at them, one might think they were standing in the open air, instead of beneath a thick layer of stone."

"So you live in a state of perpetual night underground?" she asked.

"On the upper levels of the city, close to the surface, there are air and light wells that let in sunlight during the day. But everywhere there are lamps, so the city is ablaze whenever light is needed. It is not as bright as the desert sun at noon, but only a madman would wish to be out in such heat!"

This did not seem to impress her at all. "So men sell their daughters into slavery so that you might have light?"

"There are no slaves in Tasnim. No…the girls are given as gifts, and I take them into my harem as concubines," Philemon said.

If anything, this only seemed to anger her further, as her eyebrows descended even lower. "Oh, and being forced to warm your bed is better than slavery."

Forced? He'd never forced a woman in his life! His concubines had come willingly to his bed. Had she forgotten what he looked like? He had no need to force women!

"My concubines were always appreciative of my attentions," he snapped.

"I'm sure they had little choice in the matter. A concubine who doesn't have her master's favour has little power in a harem, and he may discard her at will. So of course she will lie through her teeth if she has to, just to keep the place she has."

For a girl so young, she seemed to have excessively strong opinions about life in a harem.

"You know nothing about my concubines!"

Her eyes blazed. "No, YOU know nothing about them. My mother was a concubine, and I grew up in the harem. Saw how they were treated. So don't tell me your concubines were happy, with wives lording it over everyone, knowing you could be cast aside at the merest whim, and there was nothing you could do about it!"

Perhaps in whatever desert sheikh's harem she had grown up in, but not in a civilised city like Tasnim. "I had no wives, and as my concubines, the girls who were given to me were under my protection. Unless they chose to marry men of the city. Then their husband became their protector. But some girls preferred the harem, for it was all they had ever known. Nida had learned to play every musical instrument she could lay her hands on, and her voice soared above them all, like an angel come to Earth. If she had to choose between a husband and her harp, she would pick the harp."

Anahita's eyes widened. "You didn't touch your concubines?"

It would have been easier to say he hadn't, but he refused to lie to her, even to protect her obvious innocence about the real ways of the world.

"I lay with those who wished it. Two in particular, Zareen and Simin, were skilled in the arts of love, and took great pleasure in practicing those arts. Why, they knew things I'd never heard of…" His mind wandered as he remembered nights spent with Zareen or Simin, or, on rare occasions, both girls together. He sobered when he realised he would probably never see them again. They would be welcomed as courtesans in any court, and never return to him or Tasnim. Finally, he said, "But you don't want me to talk about concubines." He didn't want to think of them, now, either. Or all that he had lost.

"You're less amusing than I had hoped, Philemon the frog," she said frostily.

He couldn't disagree, so he racked his brain for something the girls had always liked. "Have you heard about the Gardens of Tasnim?"

Twenty-One

Anahita couldn't stop laughing. "Why would anyone want a jewelled garden? Why not plants? Trees for shade and flowers for scent…precious metals and jewels have no scent!"

"Plant do not grow underground, you see. Most plants, anyway. There are mushrooms growing in one of the lower caverns, I believe. They fetch quite a high price in the markets, or so I'm told."

Anahita knew little about mushrooms, unless they found their way into her food.

"Are you sure you're not a mushroom merchant pretending to be a prince?" she asked.

The frog drew himself up, and bumped his head on the lip of the water bag. "I assure you I am the Prince of Tasnim, and as such, it is my business to know as much as I can about my city and how to help it prosper. The mushrooms have a terrible smell, and must be kept away from where people sleep, or they complain. So the mushroom caverns are surrounded by store rooms."

Anahita couldn't imagine her father knew as much about his own city as Philemon knew about Tasnim.

"What sort of prince tells his people where they can live, or grow mushrooms? I thought there were advisers and officials who took care of such things," Anahita said.

"My father was more lenient about such things – letting people choose for themselves, and move if they needed to, but the city is more populous now, or it was, so after numerous cases where I had to judge in favour of one or the other of the city's residents, I assigned an official to take care of things." He hesitated, before continuing in a rush, "One of my concubines, if you must know."

"A woman holding office in a city? How is this possible? Surely no man would accept the judgement of a woman — and a concubine, at that!"

He made a sound of disgust. "Tasnim is not like other desert cities. Our women are not nothing. Tasnim was a garrison city, and some of the garrison were women — some say the fabled Amazons from the east. They fought and died like men, and were accorded the same citizenship when the city became a sovereign principality, no longer beholden to the fallen ancient empire who had brought together soldiers from such distant parts. My own great grandmother ruled as Princess Regent until her son came of age to claim the throne as his own.

"Rahat was one of the women given to me, who did not wish to remain in the harem. I believe she ran her father's household before she came to me, and after listening to several days' petitions, she informed me that I needed to do something about regulating my city. And she volunteered for the role. Any citizen of Tasnim who had a problem – man or woman – with her judgements could still appeal to me, but I cannot recall a single time that I judged against Rahat. She was terrifying. I found out much later that the decision to hand her over to the city to pay for the hospitality of her father's caravan was hers – and that her father was most upset when he discovered it."

Now he'd piqued her curiosity. "Did she not have a husband?"

"Actually, she did. She was quite partial to a particular kind of pastry that one of my palace cooks specialised in, and she married him. I gave her a set of golden bracelets as a wedding gift. She wore them always, and the clinking sound of them terrified many, I am told."

"You allowed your concubine to marry your cook?"

The frog waved his hands emphatically. "She was never truly a concubine, not in the way you mean the word. And she was a city official, a citizen, mistress of her own destiny. I could have challenged the marriage, but only if

I'd wished to press my own suit and marry her instead. Rahat would have turned me down flat, in any case."

"What of her father?"

The frog shrugged. "He surrendered her to me, along with any right he had to decide her future. Unwillingly, as it later turned out, but by that time it was too late. Rahat made sure of that." He smiled. "To the enduring benefit of Tasnim, I must admit."

"Who lived there? Aside from you and your concubines-who-weren't-really-concubines. And your cook."

"Merchants, mostly. Men who used their share of Tasnim's wealth to go into trade, financing caravans who were entitled to the hospitality of the city at no charge, because they were owned by the city's merchants. Women who chose to marry men in the city, rather than leave the city and risk falling into the hands of a husband who would not be as civilised as the men of Tasnim. Others chose to go into business on their own. I believe the mushroom merchants were two sisters, come to think of it."

"I would like to visit Tasnim. It sounds…nice." An impossible dream is what it sounded like. And yet…from Philemon's words, it sounded very real. She needed to see it with her own eyes to believe such a place could exist. Where women could choose…

"When you visit, you will stay there as my honoured guest," the frog promised.

Oh, she wanted to believe it so much. "And what if I do not wish to leave?"

The frog spread his arms wide. "Then you will need to find a way to earn your keep until you attain citizenship. Take up a trade, perhaps, or marry one of the city's citizens. The men of Tasnim value a good cook over a pretty face, for beauty fades." He held up his hands in supplication. "Not that you have anything to worry about. A plain woman such as yourself could never be considered just a pretty face."

Plain. If even a frog called her plain, there was no hope for Anahita. Of course, she knew her beauty did not compare to Maram or some of Father's more favoured wives, but that didn't make it hurt any less.

She had nothing to offer Tasnim. A plain face and no skill at cooking. As for a trade…all she knew how to do was hunt.

"Is there a place in Tasnim for hunters who are good at hawking?" Anahita asked.

"The mews in Tasnim has been empty for as long as I can remember. No falconer could keep the birds happy in an underground city, I understand. The job is yours, if you wish it."

For a moment, hope blossomed in her chest. A life with only her birds to care for — no husband, no harem, nothing but hunting. But her father would never allow it.

But if he did not know…believed her happily married to some sheikh…

Then and there, Anahita made a vow to herself. She would help the frog break the curse — even if she had to enlist Maram's help to find and persuade the enchantress to do so — and make Tasnim her home.

She would finally be free.

Twenty-Two

"You know what he's after, don't you?" Asad asked in a low voice as he helped Anahita unsaddle the camels.

"Who? Haidar? Of course. He wants the impossible – to turn back time," Anahita said. "To have his wife back."

"Not Haidar. The frog. The one who rides with you, and fills your ears with tales of old," Asad said.

"Philemon wants to break the curse, and go home to Tasnim." After listening to him for so many days in the desert, she knew that for a certainty, for all his tales were of Tasnim, the magical city where a woman could be more than property.

"He wants you to do it."

Anahita stared. "You're wrong. He's never asked for any such thing. He only wants me to take him to where he can find the enchantress who cursed him so she removes the curse."

"Just because he hasn't asked you yet, doesn't mean he doesn't want it. It's well known that a kiss from a princess can break most curses."

Anahita burst out laughing. "In stories, maybe. But I have never heard of such a thing happening in real life."

Asad shrugged. "Ask him, then, for heavens know you're the only one who understands the croaking sounds he makes. If anyone knows how to break his curse, it's the frog."

"He says he's a prince."

Asad snorted. "If you had to ask a pretty girl for a kiss, wouldn't you say you were a prince instead of some lowly camel herder?"

"Yes, but..." What if he was a camel herder? Would that make a difference? He talked about Tasnim with the familiarity of someone who had lived there all his life. To hear Philemon say it, though, even the lowliest citizen of Tasnim could still invite her to stay inside the city as a guest…and once inside, she could lay claim to her place as the prince's falconer. "I'm sure I'm not important enough for a kiss from me to work. Besides, I don't think he even knows I am a princess, high or low. And I don't want you telling him, either!"

It was Asad's turn to laugh. "No man needs to be told. The uppity way you carry yourself and order everyone about tells the world what you are."

Anahita dropped the saddle, sending up a cloud of dust that made her cough. It took a long moment for the coughing fit to subside, before she said, "Oh yes, and I'm sure princesses regularly take care of the camels whenever they travel. If I were Maram, I'd stand by impatiently, tapping my foot, until my pavilion was ready for me, and retire in there, where my servants tended to my every need!"

"Haidar would do it, if you asked him. He'd set up your tent and help you wash, quite happily."

He would, too. But Anahita would not torture her friend so with what could never be. "I'd sooner order you to start making a meal for us. And he didn't call me pretty. In fact, he regularly tells me how plain I am."

"Then your frog's a fool. But I'd be an even bigger fool if I let you cook. I'll tell you what. I'll wager the new knife I bought in the market before we left – the one with the emerald set into the handle – that he asks you for a kiss before we reach the sheikh's camp."

Anahita eyed the water bag where Philemon travelled by day, but he'd hopped over to the shallow pool of fresh water where Haidar was filling up the water jars.

"If you're wrong, I get the knife. If you're right…I'll have a second such knife crafted to match the first, as my gift to you when we get home." And they would go home, Anahita added silently to herself.

Asad rubbed his hands. "An easy bet, I'm sure. You know what else is a foregone conclusion? What you'll do when he asks you."

Was she so transparent? Asad's assertion

had taken her by such surprise that even Anahita wasn't sure what she'd do. "What, then?" she asked finally.

"You'll feed the frog to your falcon, of course. Your father may not know it, but we do – you'll never let another man touch you again. And he might be a frog now, but whatever else he is, that one's a man." Asad jerked his chin up. "Your bird's back. Looks like she has dinner, too, so I'd better get the fire going." He headed off.

Anahita watched Merlin glide gracefully to land at her feet, before the bird laid her catch out proudly. A scurrier of some sort, and a small one, at that. Not enough to feed one, let alone three of them. Asad could cook something from their provisions tonight. "You eat it. Maybe next oasis will have more ducks."

"Or frogs!" the falcon said, neatly eviscerating her prey.

At least the bird had forgotten about Philemon, for the moment. Anahita wished she could do the same. Because despite Asad's assertion, she wasn't as sure she'd refuse him if Philemon asked her to help him break the curse. Usually the journey through the desert dragged, but with him to talk to and tell stories of the wonders of the city he loved so much, the week had flown by. She'd thought his overweening pride would have put her off, but somehow…she'd grown used to it. Maybe even liked him.

So if he asked for her help…could she, in conscience, refuse? A kiss was such a small thing, really.

Twenty-Three

From his perch atop a camel's back, safely wedged into the neck of a water bag, Philemon watched the three of them set up camp, like he had every night since he'd joined their small caravan. Haidar refilled their water supply and Asad built a fire and began to cook. Anahita sent her bird off hunting while she pitched the tent and carried their bedrolls into it, so that they might sleep comfortably. If they hadn't stopped at an oasis, Haidar would help her with the tent.

Anahita's eyes often followed the falcon's

flight, while she wore a wistful expression, as if she wished she could fly with the diabolical bird.

For the first time, he wondered what her story was. He wished he'd spent less time talking and taken the time to ask her about herself. He knew she was an experienced desert traveller, and the way she and her brothers divided up the tasks in camp so easily, she must travel with them often. She might not know it, but she was freer than any desert woman he'd ever met – including those who lived in Tasnim, for the women of his city had mostly stayed within the underground city. For all their freedom, Tasnim citizens did not spend much time staring at the sky, or even standing beneath it.

Every morning she lifted him from his bucket and into the water bag, never once flinching at his slimy skin. It wasn't that she didn't notice, either – her brothers had made comments on how they would not carry frogs as she did. She'd smiled, shrugged, and thrown a teasing comment right back at the brother in question, but she hadn't let him go.

He'd found himself racking his brain to tell her tales he hadn't shared yet — half-remembered events from his childhood, or tales of the history of Tasnim, which she'd never heard. He'd even found himself telling her about his journey through the dark to the oasis, and discovering he'd been turned into a frog. So what if he'd made it sound like a glorious adventure, instead of the nightmarish reality? Her eyes had still grown wide before she'd laughed in all the right places.

More than anything, he wanted to take her home to Tasnim, and show her all the wonders his words simply couldn't describe.

But first he would have to find a way to break the curse, and return the waters to his city. Otherwise there would be nothing but empty caverns to show her, before her bird tried to eat him again.

If only her brothers had brought her sooner, and tried to trade her for Tasnim's hospitality. Then he might have persuaded her to become one of his concubines…

Though he suspected she would refuse the honour. If her brothers had been willing to part with her, which seemed equally unlikely.

It was a foolish thought, he told himself. Better to focus on breaking this curse, and claiming his princess bride from the Sultan. Whatever beauty the Sultan bestowed on him would surely be enough to turn his thoughts away from a barbarian girl, chance met in the desert. A girl as unattainable as the rising moon.

"Will you join us for dinner, Philemon?"

Philemon roused himself from his gloomy thoughts to find Anahita standing before him, her cupped hands ready to carry him.

He could not smell the stew already steaming over the fire behind her, but he didn't need to smell it to know it would taste far better than any meal he'd eaten since that enchantress pushed him down the well. But the fire had probably drawn an inordinate number of bugs by its light, and Anahita wished him to take care of them.

"I'm not sure you'll like that," he said, stepping into her hands. "Watching a frog crunch through a bug while it's still alive is enough to put the strongest man off his food."

"I guess my stomach is stronger than that of most men. But then, I've watched my birds rip their prey apart for as long as I can remember."

Philemon shuddered. "Where is the creature?"

"Merlin is hunting. She says there are a large number of fat frogs in this oasis, and she intends to catch them all." Anahita ducked her head. "I thought you might prefer to stay with us, where she does not mistake you for food."

Ah, so she didn't want her dinner interrupted by having to rescue him from the bird again. If Philemon could but carry a blade at his hip, he would soon see the bird off, but neither Anahita or her brothers had a knife small enough to serve him as a sword.

"You are fortunate that I am a prince and not truly a frog, or I would take offence at the bird's slaughter of my family," Philemon said. "For honour's sake, I would be forced to kill the bird, and all who harbour it."

Anahita shook her head. "And that's why I know you're not truly a frog. Animals do not say such things, or care about honour. I still imagine it would be distressing to see the slaughter of your fellow creatures, especially with your human sensibilities."

She set him on a rug beside the fire. He had barely a moment to notice that it was the rug she usually draped atop her bedroll before his body seemed to sneeze again.

"He's too skinny to be a prince. Pampered princes are plumper than that," a male voice said.

It took Philemon a moment to collect his scattered wits before he realised the man meant to insult him. He leaped to his feet. "Plump or skinny, a prince defends his honour. Give me a blade and I will make you regret every word."

Someone threw a bundle of cloth at him. "Put some clothes on, so you don't put Ana off her dinner."

Philemon caught it, and he was stunned to find his own hands holding the bundle, instead of his four-fingered frog ones. "By what miracle…" he began.

"Ana's idea. Last time you turned into a man, it was in her bed. She figured it was worth a try. I bet it would work. Asad said it wouldn't. I'll share the wineskin I won off him with you if you can tell me why. Ana insists there's nothing magical about her bed, but she doesn't usually share it with animals."

Philemon shook his head. "I know not. I have never been cursed before. And if I can break this one…I hope never to be cursed again." Realisation dawned. "You can hear me. Understand me."

Haidar nodded. "Well enough to see Ana isn't telling tales about you being a man under some spell." He lowered his voice. "Put the robe on, and she'll come closer. Naked men frighten her."

Philemon's gaze followed Haidar's pointing finger to where Anahita stood, at the very edge of the firelight. The reflected flames glittered in her eyes and off her teeth as she bit her lip. Contrary to her brother's words, there was no fear in her expression.

She stalked forward, as graceful as any desert hunting cat. By the time she stepped between Philemon and the fire, he had eyes for nothing but her.

The firelight turned her thin tunic transparent, highlighting the curves it otherwise might have hidden. Beautiful. Like an angel come to earth. He wanted to say the words aloud, but his mouth was too dry for any sound to come out.

He lifted his gaze to meet her eyes, but found them downcast. Not to the ground, but to his groin. Because a prince's cock refused to bow down to a beautiful woman. Instead, it rose to greet her. Ready.

For something her wary eyes said she would never agree to.

Philemon sighed and slipped the robe over his head, hiding his arousal as he tried to think of anything but the beautiful girl before him. Beautiful. Untouchable. Unless he was a frog, when she took him in her hands and…

"Will the spell object if I sit beside you? Or will you turn back into a frog?"

Philemon's eyes sprang open to find Anahita sinking to her knees before him. No, beside him on the bedroll, close enough to touch if he took his place beside her. A place she patted, a playful expression on her face.

"I rarely bite, Philemon. Except when it's my dinner." She accepted a bowl from Asad.

"Sit down, and hide that tent in your tunic," Asad muttered, shoving a second bowl at Philemon.

Philemon did as he was told, telling himself that if he'd had a sister as irresistible as Anahita, he would be just as protective.

But she sat close enough for him to feel the heat of her through his thin robe, while her brothers sat on the other side of the fire, their eyes fixed on Philemon. Torture. Temptation. Both terrible and yet...

"You should have left the stew to cook for longer. The meat is tougher than I like," Anahita said.

Asad shrugged. "Use your dagger to cut it into smaller pieces. Or don't eat it. It is all the same to me."

Anahita's arm bumped his side. "What do you think, Philemon? Do you agree that Asad did not cook the lamb enough?"

Philemon turned his attention to his food. He spooned up some of the stew and brought it to his lips. The sauce was well spiced and salted, but so was the meat. Spiced lamb as good as anything he'd tasted in Tasnim. He owned it was a little chewy, but no more so than any slice of roast lamb he'd eaten in the past. Right now, it might as well have been manna from heaven, it tasted so good. Before he'd realised it, he'd finished the bowl. "Is there more?" he asked.

Too late did he realise that Anahita and her brothers might not have enough food to satisfy him, especially after so long eating like a frog.

Asad scraped a spoon through the pot, eyeing Philemon across the fire. "Maybe," Asad said slowly. "What price would you pay me for it?"

Anahita hushed him. "Philemon is our guest. It breaks the laws of hospitality to expect a guest to pay for a meal we invited him to."

"To hear you tell it, he claims to be the Prince of Tasnim. Do you know how much it costs for the privilege of a bowl of lamb stew in Tasnim?" Asad asked.

A man who drove a hard bargain. Philemon

could respect that. "I will trade one for the other. A meal at my table in Tasnim, for a meal here at yours." He glanced around. "A meal for all of you, with as much of my best wine as you wish."

Asad wiped his hands. "Take note, Ana. No man of Tasnim would pay such a price for a simple meal, let alone a prince. I don't know who your frog man is, but he is not who he claims to be. A meal in Tasnim costs a prince's ransom. If he'd tossed me a gold coin for stew that would cost him two coppers in the capital, I'd have believed him." He bowed mockingly in Philemon's direction. "Perhaps you will have more luck fooling the next caravan who offer to help you. I am going to go water the dunes, and I will be a while." He marched off into the darkness, muttering under his breath.

Haidar rose from his seat and peered into the pot. "There is plenty left, if you want it. No matter what he says, Asad is as hospitable as the rest of us. It's yours." He held out the spoon.

Philemon rose and stepped forward to accept it.

On his second step, the world constricted to crush him.

Twenty-Four

Anahita watched in stunned horror as Philemon's robe fluttered to the sand, seemingly empty but for a tiny bulge she knew had to be his frog body, especially when it moved. She rushed forward and scooped him up, robe and all, then dropped him back on her bedroll. She wasn't sure what magic let him become a man there, but she intended to find out. She might not be an enchantress, but she still was a witch, even if all she could do was understand animals.

Though understanding Philemon was

proving quite a challenge. She'd never met a frog like him – or a man like him, either.

The robe ballooned out as the magic in him turned him into a man again, or at least she hoped so. Philemon groaned.

"I'm going to check on the camels," Haidar said pointedly. "Like Asad, I will be a while."

Anahita didn't pay him more than a fleeting glance and a distracted nod as she patted down the robe to find the man she hoped was inside. He felt…normal.

A sigh of relief whooshed out of her as his head emerged from the neck of the robe. "Thank heavens," she breathed.

Philemon sat up suddenly, and his face was dangerously close to hers. It was now or never.

Anahita took a deep breath, then pressed her lips to his.

Please let this kiss break the curse, she prayed to anyone who was listening.

For a second, they stayed there like that, before Philemon leaned back and broke the contact between them. "What was that?" he asked.

Her heart sank. "A kiss, of course. Asad

thinks that a kiss from me might break your curse, and as we arrive at our destination tomorrow, you might appreciate being able to walk around and talk to people as a man again, as I will not be as...available."

"Yes, I have heard that women can be quite busy at weddings. Especially if they are close to the bride," Philemon said drily.

Anahita wet her lips. Dare she tell him the truth? No, she could not risk it. "Yes, I am close to her. So if I can help you break the curse, it must be tonight."

"You must kiss me tonight?"

Curse him, it almost sounded like he was holding back laughter.

"I already did," she snapped.

He did laugh then, a rich sound that echoed off the dunes. Nothing like the reedy voice of a frog. It did things to her belly. "That wasn't a kiss. Definitely not something a spell would recognise."

Anahita pouted. "What sort of kiss does a spell recognise? Tell me and I shall do it."

"I don't know for certain, never having broken a spell with one before, but I imagine a kiss with the power to break spells would need some passion behind it. You'd need both your heart and soul in it. And your tongue."

"My tongue?" What was she supposed to do with her tongue? Lick him? Desperately, Anahita wished she'd brought Maram along. She knew about kissing, and such things. For all her husbands, Anahita had never kissed a man in her life. This idea was rapidly turning into a terrible one. But if she could break the curse, she had to do it tonight. For tomorrow would be too late. "Very well."

His face loomed close – almost too close – and he lifted a hand to her cheek. Not to capture her, like other men might have. No, his fingers brushed against her hair as his palm cupped her jaw, sensing she needed the support or reassurance. Leaving her free to flee if she needed to.

But she did not need to, Anahita scolded herself and her racing heart. Why, even her breath was coming fast now.

His thumb traced her lips. The top one, then the bottom, as she forced herself to exhale slowly.

"Don't be afraid," he said softly.

She wasn't afraid. She wasn't. By all that was holy…

Then his lips touched hers, and she forgot all else.

He inhaled, stealing her breath, before sealing his mouth to hers. Her mouth opened almost of its own accord, her lips following his. And then his tongue stroked hers, a teasing invitation to come out to play.

She wasn't afraid.

She cupped his face in her hands, and kissed him back with all of her being. Tongue, lips, breath, heart…maybe even her very soul. Clumsily at first, but when he didn't seem to care, she grew bolder, opening her eyes and raising them to meet his.

And she was lost. Utterly and completely lost, yet found, never wanting to stop…

"Ana. Ana!"

Who was calling her name at such a moment?

"Breathe, Ana."

Her face was pressed against a broad chest as a tender hand stroked her hair.

She sucked in a breath, then another, relishing the taste of him on her lips, her tongue. The heat of him, so close.

"Philemon, why did you stop?" she asked.

Laughter rumbled beneath her cheek. "What do you think your brothers would do if they knew you'd kissed a frog with such passion you'd forgotten to breathe?"

Her brothers? Anahita flicked her fingers. "Nothing, I'm sure. They hardly know I exist, so I'm sure they would not care what happens to me."

"Not so. Haven't they been watching us all evening? I'm sure Asad and Haidar care very much about you. So much that if they knew what we had just done, they would happily bury me alive in a desert grave before dawn."

It was her turn to laugh. "Asad and Haidar aren't my brothers! They're my father's sworn men!"

Haidar's voice came out of the dark. "Your sworn eunuchs!"

Philemon stiffened.

"Sworn to protect me," Anahita amended. "Ready to come at my call, should I need their help."

Philemon eased away from her. "Men who would happily remove a frog from your bed. I should find my own bed, or bucket." He rose.

Anahita grabbed his arm. "No! If any kiss can break a curse, that one should have done so. Surely. You should sleep here. I will take some of the spare cushions and things in the tent. Or take Asad's bedroll. He often complains it is too soft for him." She bit her lip, unable to tear her eyes away from his. Philemon looked so…so sad. "Tell me that kiss was enough!"

He sighed. "One kiss from you will never be enough, and yet, it must be. But yes, if any kiss had curse-breaking powers, it was yours." He pried her hand from his arm. "I thank you for your hospitality tonight, and pray that your dreams are sweet."

Her dreams were never sweet. Especially not the night before she married. Anahita turned away before Philemon could see her grimace.

"Sweet dreams to you, too, Philemon," she called over her shoulder with forced lightness as she trudged to the tent where she hoped she might get some sleep tonight.

Twenty-Five

"Oh no!" The feminine wail woke Philemon from what had been a sound sleep.

He scrambled out of the covers and blinked in the blazing sun. He'd missed the dawn, this time. Possibly because the blankets on Anahita's bed had blocked it out. "What is it?" he mumbled, wishing his mouth didn't taste like the inside of someone else's sweaty sandal. He'd drunk too much wine last night.

"The curse didn't break!" Already on her knees, she stretched her hands out to Philemon, and he stepped onto them without thinking.

"No," he agreed. He hadn't the heart to break it to her that the only kisses capable of breaking curses came from princesses, and this desert girl wasn't capable of fooling a curse into believing she was royalty when she wasn't. Besides, the witch had said something about a princess's bed being the key. Perhaps Anahita's bedroll had once belonged to some minor princess before someone stole it for her.

He was damn sure that he'd given Anahita her first kiss. He'd meant to make it quick and light, but the moment her natural passion had asserted itself, pushing aside her initial awkwardness, he hadn't been able to let her go. It had been like drowning, with her lips breathing life into him for the first time. And yet, they'd been so intent on each other, they'd forgotten to breathe.

"You don't have time for that today. You need to get dressed, so we can head out," Haidar said, holding out the water bag Philemon usually rode in.

Philemon hopped into the cool water. Darkness engulfed him as someone stoppered the bag, but he wasn't worried. He'd push the stopper out once he felt the sway of the camel beneath him, when they were under way.

In the meantime, he dreamed of Anahita's kisses, and how he might manage to keep her forever.

The bag lurched to one side, then back, water sloshing around Philemon as the camel rose cumbrously to its feet. The ride began bumpily at first, until the camel settled into a steady pace. Finally.

Philemon set his shoulder against the stopper, pushing until he felt it pop free.

"So what does a frog have to promise a lady to be invited to her table again tonight?" he asked, peering up.

Haidar shook his head. "I don't speak frog, so save your croaking. Her Highness has no time for pets today. Even her precious bird rides with Asad."

Philemon leaned out further so that he might see the truth of Haidar's words. Before them rode Asad, with the bird on a perch strapped to his saddle. And behind them…

Philemon swallowed. The white veiled

desert maiden was no more. Instead, she wore the colours of the desert, a bright reddish orange stiff with gold embroidery that made her glitter in the sun. The rich robe draped over the saddle so extravagantly that the silk hid both her and the saddle completely. As the sun rose higher, the cloth canopy above her would shelter her from its heat, but now the only shadow it cast landed on her face, so he could not even see her eyes.

She looked like some desert queen out of legend, ready to lead an army into immortality. No, to accept a defeated army's surrender. Dressed so, she was clearly no warrior. Her Highness…so she was a princess after all? Or was it all a pretence?

A stolen bedroll, stolen clothes…was she a pretend princess, or a very real one? He wanted to ask, but Haidar would not understand him.

Philemon stared at the regal statue that had to be Anahita for a moment longer before he retreated back into his water bag, pulling the stopper into place behind him.

Twenty-Six

Muffled shouting as the camels drew to a halt caught Philemon's attention first. The rough descent as his camel sank to its knees confirmed it. They'd arrived somewhere. Their destination, perhaps? A long moment passed, but no one unloaded his water bag, so he pushed at the stopper to peep at his surroundings.

A desert nomad camp stretched out across the sand, brightly coloured tents huddled together against the surrounding dunes. The men who had assembled to greet the small caravan wore clothing as patched as the tents. Despite its size, this was not a prosperous camp.

A clinking sound drew everyone's attention away from the new arrivals.

Could it be Rahat?

The crowd parted to let a man through. A man who looked like he'd raided his mother's jewel chest and had no idea how ridiculous he looked, wearing his mother's treasures. Gold bangles covered his forearms, and countless gold chains weighed down his thick neck, some of them dangling as low as his protruding belly. The silk robe he wore looked like he'd stolen it from some courtesan, for surely no one else would wear such a garish shade of purple. Except perhaps a fool in the Sultan's court.

But no man knelt before a jester, like these were now. Whoever this fool was, no one dared mock him.

Even Haidar and Asad, who stepped forward to press their foreheads to the dust at the man's feet.

"Most Honoured Sheikh Basit, we bring a

gift from the Sultan. Your bride, Her Highness, Princess Anahita."

Anahita's camel was the only one still standing, so she towered above all of them, including – Philemon swallowed back bile – her incensed future husband.

"A good, obedient bride does not sit higher than her husband. She must abase herself," the sheikh announced.

Philemon smirked. Anahita wasn't the abasing kind. This would be interesting.

Asad and Haidar rose and headed for Anahita. A command from Asad made the camel kneel, so that Anahita could dismount, but the girl didn't move. Instead, Asad and Haidar each took one of her arms and lifted her off the beast, carried her several feet, then deposited her on the sand. Her robe puddled around her feet, spreading into a train that swept along the sand behind her as she crossed the distance between her and her hideous husband-to-be.

To Philemon's astonishment, she dropped to her knees, then threw herself facedown on the sand.

The sheikh smiled. Then he lifted his slippered foot and brought it down on her neck.

Philemon gasped, but no one heard. He wanted to storm across the sand and shove the sheikh away from her, but as a frog, he couldn't do anything.

So much for Haidar and Asad claiming to be her sworn men. They weren't anything of the kind – a man sworn to protect her would have killed the sheikh by now, yet he still stood there, ready to break her neck with one stomp of his foolish foot. They really were eunuchs.

Was this why Anahita had tried so hard to break the curse last night? So that he could help her, when no one else would? No wonder she'd despaired when she discovered her kisses hadn't worked. She knew the fate that awaited her.

Poor girl. Philemon couldn't begin to imagine what thoughts were going through Anahita's mind at that moment. Of one thing he was certain: she must be terrified.

Twenty-Seven

If she slipped a blade out of her wrist sheath, she could reach up and sever his Achilles tendon. Both of them, if she was quick. Throw a handful of sand in his eyes as she jumped to her feet, and run. Anahita's instincts urged her to do just that, but she knew she could not. Not yet. For if half the marketplace gossip about this man was true…she could not risk leaving him alive.

Running could wait until after the deed was done. Until then, cold calculation would occupy her mind, as it always did. Haidar and

Asad had taught her well.

In the meantime, she allowed herself the small fantasy of choking him with the very shoe he'd balanced on the back of her neck. Watching his face grow red, then purple, then blue as he gasped for air that would never again reach his lungs...

"Take her to the women's tent, where they can prepare her for our wedding. If she pleases me tonight, you can carry word back to your master on the morrow. If she does not..." The foot pressed against her neck, making it hard to breathe. "Perhaps I will make her head MY gift to the Sultan, and the next gift the Sultan sends will be more acceptable."

The sheikh did not know how wrong he was, but Anahita had no desire to enlighten him just yet. His time would come, and she would enjoy it. For now, she forced her face to appear blank as Haidar and Asad took her arms and hauled her to her feet. She itched to brush the dust off her embroidered gown, but that, too, could wait. Some servant could deal with the damage when she returned home. She would not wear this again, if she could help it.

She would have enough to do, finding another way to break Philemon's curse. Once this current task was complete. First, she had to grind Basit's face in the dirt.

Asad thrust her through the flap of the largest tent in the camp, from blazing light into darkness. It took her a moment for her eyes to adjust, which was time enough for Haidar to drop a bag of her things at her feet and inform the women of their sheikh's orders for her.

Then the tent flap closed entirely, leaving her alone with what looked like a hundred women, curious about the newest of their number.

Anahita relaxed. She knew her place in a harem – even this one. She allowed the women to lift her dusty robe off, and pretended not to notice their exclamations at the quality of the work or the quantity of dust on it.

"She's so small!"

"He'll break her on her first time."

"She looks terrified."

"Such a pretty tunic. Are the jewels real?"

Anahita let their words wash over her, not uttering a word except to nod occasionally if someone asked her a question. A new bride in a new home was supposed to be nervous. Never mind that she outranked all of them — once she married their sheikh, her place would be his to dictate. So she surrendered to them for now.

"Should we tell her? Warn her, maybe?"

"Can't risk it."

"She should save herself if she can. What if she suffers the same fate as Inbal?"

Inbal, a girl who could not have been older than ten, Anahita discovered, had had her tongue cut out for saying something that displeased the sheikh.

Anahita resolved to avenge the girl.

"Make her so beautiful he cannot resist."

"Oh, isn't the silk lovely? So fine, you can see quite through it!"

"That will not last the night."

Women washed her with cool water, then applied perfumed oils to her skin, before helping her into her wedding clothes — the contents of the bags Haidar had brought. Sheer silk so thin that in the right light, you could see through it, but only her husband would see that, in the privacy of his tent tonight. She fastened the bells onto her bracelets herself, while two small girls did the same with her anklets. A thin chain of bells clipped to her belt, and her dance clothes were complete.

"Do you think they will succeed?"

"They must! This cannot go on."

"Don't forget to oil her hair. You know how grabby his hands can be. At least give her a chance."

They combed, curled and oiled her hair, a luxury Anahita had not allowed herself while they travelled. Hair oil seemed to pick up every speck of dust in the desert, but tonight its glossy sheen would catch the light once she took her veil off. She knew she was too plain to attract him with her beauty – even Philemon had said so.

"Wish we dared poison the wedding feast. He and his favourites alone will eat it – this poor mite won't eat a bite."

"Better that way. What would he do to her if she vomited her food at his feet?"

"Don't even think it. Whoever does the

deed will have my thanks."

"And mine."

"Who is it, do you know?"

"One of the men. They all want the honour of delivering the final blow."

"Of course they do. They know what it means."

Over the gossamer silk, they placed another heavily embroidered robe the blood-red colour of her marriage bed. Jewels had been sewn into this one – dark rubies that glittered in the light, drawing attention to the curve of her breasts beneath it.

"When will it happen?"

"After the feast, when he takes her to his bed."

"Actually IN…?"

"Shh, she looks scared enough. Don't frighten her further. It must be tonight."

The matching jewelled veil completed her bridal clothes, covering Anahita's hair and all but her eyes.

"Doesn't she look a vision?"

"He will not be able to resist."

"Good."

A gentle hand landed on Anahita's shoulder, and she met the pitying eyes of an older woman. "It's all right to be afraid, chick. All brides fear their wedding night. Just stay silent, lie back, and submit to whatever he wishes. It will be over quickly."

Anahita's heart sank as the woman didn't say the final line of bridal advice she'd heard so many times in her father's harem: "You might even enjoy it." No one here enjoyed Sheikh Basit's attentions.

No wonder they were plotting a coup tonight.

A coup that could not succeed if the sheikh was already dead at her hands.

Did she have the right to take vengeance away from these women? Stolen from their fathers, husbands, families, to serve his pleasure?

Ah, but none of the women would deliver the blow. And she had her answer.

She didn't need a man to save her. Anahita would save herself. And all of them. The moment that arsehole put his foot on her neck, he'd sealed his fate.

Twenty-Eight

Philemon sat, forgotten, with the camels and other animals. Would this be his fate forever? Even the passionate kiss of the princess he loved had not been able to break the curse. If Anahita couldn't do it, then could anyone? Or would he be alone forever?

The sounds of feasting and merriment came from a well-lit tent near the middle of the encampment, beside the women's tent where they'd taken Anahita. Women walked between the two, carrying platters of food or what remained of it after the men had devoured everything.

He hadn't heard a single female voice since he arrived, he realised. No laughter, no chatter – none of the normal sounds he'd expect from normal women. They might be more outspoken in Tasnim than other places, but nowhere had he ever met women who were forced into silence. It was against their very natures. There was something very wrong in this camp, and he wished he were far from it. But he could not leave Anahita here among the worst of it. With that sheikh who didn't deserve to kiss the ground she walked upon.

Whose wedding feast they were no doubt celebrating now. A feast to give the bridegroom stamina, for the true test of a wedding was whether he could keep the bride in his tent until morning, when the wedding breakfast they shared concluded the marriage ceremony.

Yesterday, he would have bet money on Anahita not staying until morning but after what he'd seen today…

Had her men drugged her? Given her something that would make her more docile?

Or cast some spell on her that had the same effect? Was that why he'd been kept away from her, and made to ride with Haidar?

He prayed they had not, but he could not be certain. Even if he was, what could he do? He was a frog.

"Are we still doing it tonight?" an unfamiliar voice whispered.

"Of course! Every day under his rule is an abomination to the honour of all good men," a second voice hissed back.

"And their wives," the first one muttered.

"Why didn't someone just poison his food?"

"Didn't you see the boys he has lined up at his feet? Their mothers cook the meals, and must feed each dish to their own sons before he tastes a single bite. That's how he foiled the first poisoning attempt. The women do not dare any more. It must be us, and we cannot fail!"

"When? There was so much arguing, I couldn't stay to find out what they decided. An ambush after the feast, when he is too drunk on wine to see it?"

"Of course not. He'll be expecting that.

Besides, did you see him drink more than a cup of wine at the feast? No, he has all his wits about him now, and he will expect an attack as he walks back to his tent with his princess. She's barely more than a child, my wife said. Would you willingly give your daughter to that monster?"

"I'd sooner kill my daughter than give her to him. It is fortunate I don't have one."

"Not yet. If you get your wife back on the morrow, I'll wager you'll be busy planting one in her belly before sundown!"

"If she still lives. She hasn't left the women's tent in weeks."

"She's the only healer left. They're probably keeping her busy, healing the girls the morning after he's had them. If he'd killed someone, we'd know about it, for who'd he send to bury her, hmm?"

"Maybe. So when will we finally be rid of him again?"

"We wait until he's distracted, deflowering his child bride, and then we strike."

"What about the girl?"

"If she gets in the way, kill her, too. No one

here will mourn her."

Philemon opened his mouth to shout that he would, but he knew it was no use. They wouldn't hear him. Only Anahita would understand him. Someone needed to warn her.

"He'll probably crush her the first time he tries to mount her. They say that's what happened to Ahmed's daughter. He broke her hip bones with his weight, and she wouldn't stop screaming, so he killed her."

"If she's screaming, he won't hear us until it's too late."

Cheers and catcalls rose from the feasting tent.

"Look out. He's heading to bed."

The plotting men disappeared into the shadows as a couple appeared on the track that ran between the tents. He held a torch aloft in one hand as his other arm encircled the waist of a girl dressed head to toe in blood red.

Anahita. It had to be.

She walked willingly, he noted – the sheikh did not need to drag her. She should be trying to tear loose from his grasp, to run away.

Philemon shouted a warning at the top of

his lungs, but she didn't seem to hear, for she kept going. To her death, he was sure of it.

Cursing his already cursed body, Philemon leaped down from the camel's back and headed after them. He had to warn her, about the monstrous sheikh and his imminent death. A warning just for her ears, for the sheikh would not understand him.

He hopped faster. He had to save her.

Twenty-Nine

It took every drop of Anahita's self control not to sink a blade into Basit's arm as he marched her away from the feasting tent. Not that she'd wanted to stay, but his meaty fingers biting into her arm would leave bruises.

Her stomach protested that she hadn't eaten, but Anahita ignored it. No one had offered her food or wine at the feast – even her previous husbands had made an effort to feed her. Then again, with Basit's greedy eyes on her, she hadn't felt like eating.

While he stuffed himself and his men drank

countless toasts to his health and virility and other such manly virtues, she'd watched the crowd. Several men had slipped out, unseen by anyone but her, and she'd witnessed whispered conversations between the serving women and some of the men seated at the lower tables.

The bloated bastard beside her was blissfully unaware of the coup his own people had planned, while she saw signs of it all around her, spreading like a sickness. Eyes watched from the darkness between the tents as they passed, but none came close enough to kill the man. No, they wanted her to distract him.

And she would, but not in the way they had planned. For she was not a pawn in anyone's game. Not her father's, not Basit's, and definitely not the strange one played by his people.

Basit shoved her through a tent flap, shouting for some guards to take their position at the entrance. Haidar and Asad, she hoped, as they'd planned.

Gaily coloured silk cushions lay in piles everywhere, not unlike Maram's bedchamber if she'd tripled the number of cushions and not cared about the colours. Or the cleanliness of them, Anahita realised, noting the stains on several of them. A patch of dried blood here, something white and crusted across two of them, something yellow that had turned part of an azure blue cushion murky green… She shuddered.

"Get your clothes off. Now," Basit growled, shoving her toward the dirty cushions.

Anahita ducked her head to hide the fury in her eyes. "In the Sultan's harem, it is traditional for a new bride to perform an intimate dance for her husband as she removes her wedding clothes. I am told it is necessary to increase a husband's pleasure."

Actually, Maram had told her it give her a way to take off her own clothes without her husband noticing how many knives she carried, but Anahita wasn't going to tell him that.

Basit threw himself on the cushions and folded his arms across his chest. "I will be the judge of that. Show me."

Anahita took a deep breath, then began to mark the beat with her feet, stamping on the ground until she had the rhythm in her head. Then she began to move, unfastening the heavy, red gown slowly as she moved her hips to swirl the skirt.

Basit grunted.

She released the last fastener and let the gown's own weight carry it to the floor, revealing the thin silk tunic she wore underneath. A twirl unfurled the skirt fully, showing off everything before the folds settled again, giving only a tantalising glimpse as she moved.

The heavy red veil was next. She turned her back as she tore the garment from her head, shaking it out so that it flew like a banner behind her as she danced. She turned to face him, revealing her face to him for the first time, and held her breath.

Plain she might be, but the women here had done their best to paint her eyes to make them look bigger, and redden her lips, too.

The obvious approval in his expression made her breathe out a sigh of relief. She danced faster, her every movement sending the bells on her belt jingling.

"Enough dancing. Take the rest off," Basit ordered.

Anahita pretended not to hear, planting her hands on her hips as she moved them again, more slow and sensuous this time.

"I said now!"

He grabbed her arm and dragged Anahita around to face him, tearing her sleeve.

Another gossamer silk tunic ruined. What was wrong with men?

Anahita met his eyes. "And I say no."

Thirty

The track between the tents seemed to stretch forever. Philemon would never get there in time to warn her. Not before that misbegotten camel herder got his hands on her…and what if he hurt her? Philemon sucked in a breath and hopped faster.

Of course the sheikh's tent was at the far end of the camp. Where no one could hear the screams of his women as he tortured them, most likely. Barbarian.

Four guards stood at the entrance. Two tribesmen, Haidar, and Asad. Philemon cursed.

He couldn't go in without her men spotting him.

He hopped around the back of the tent, looking for another way in. Maybe if he squeezed under the tent wall here, digging under it a little, he might manage…

A woman's scream sliced through the night. Then another. From inside the tent.

Anahita.

He squeezed through the gap, not caring what happened to him, and caught sight of Anahita struggling with the sheikh.

He had to stop him. Couldn't let him hurt her.

But what could a frog do?

He eyed the sea of cushions between him and the woman he loved.

Her marriage bed.

He'd make Basit rue even looking at Anahita.

Philemon leaped.

Thirty-One

Anahita started to scream, startling Basit into releasing her. She didn't hesitate, thrusting her knife up to pierce his throat. Once, twice, then a third time. Basit jerked his head up, ripping the blade from her hand, before she could deliver a final blow.

Gasping for air he could no longer breathe, Basit fell heavily against her, nearly knocking her over. Anahita fought to stay on her feet, then to push him off her. He weighed so much, but she gave an almighty heave and she was free. He tumbled back onto his soiled cushions.

Beside a naked man.

Philemon?

She opened his mouth to ask how, or perhaps why…

The guards chose that moment to charge into the tent.

Anahita thought fast.

"He killed him! He killed him!" she screamed, pointing at Philemon, as she backed into a corner of the tent and curled up into what she hoped looked like a hysterical wife pushed past what her mind could handle without going mad.

Haidar and Asad would seize him, he'd turn back into a frog, and chaos would ensue. She could retrieve her knife, and slip off into the darkness. Though if she had time, she'd still like to cut out his tongue.

"You killed the sheikh?" one of Basit's men asked shakily.

Philemon drew himself up to his full height. "I did. Honour demanded it."

Anahita suppressed a snort. There was nothing honourable about Basit's death. She'd made certain of that.

In the silence that followed, she risked another look. Basit's men had dropped to their knees, pressing their foreheads to the floor. Asad and Haidar slowly followed their example.

"Honoured Sheikh, what are your orders?" one man asked.

Philemon's mouth opened, but no words came out.

Anahita wasn't as familiar with desert politics as Maram, but she vaguely remembered something about tribes where leadership was won by being the strongest fighter, and the succession was not by birth, but by force of arms. Kill the leader, and you inherited his position. Was it like that here?

Asad seemed to think so. "Most Honoured Sheikh, would you like us to bring you a better wife to warm your bed? One who is not so…hysterical?" He nodded in Anahita's direction.

She buried her head in her hands again and whimpered a little. Her throat was already sore from screaming – she didn't want to do it any more tonight, if she didn't have to.

"This one will suit me fine. I'm sure she will calm as soon as you remove the corpse from her chamber," Philemon said. "And bring us fresh bedding."

"As you command, Most Honoured Sheikh," they chorused.

Anahita's hands clenched into fists. When she got Philemon alone, she would throttle him for this. This wasn't her plan at all.

Thirty-Two

The guards took an eternity to carry all the cushions out of the tent, or so it seemed, before they set up a bedroll big enough for a bridal couple.

Two men rolled the former sheikh in the blood-soaked carpet beneath him, then lifted the grisly bundle between them.

"Wait!" A third man made them set their burden down and open it.

By all that was holy, why? Philemon wanted to scream.

The third man pulled the knife from the

sheikh's breast, wiped the bloodied blade on his own robes, then held it out to Philemon. "Your blade, Honoured Sheikh."

It was a pledge of fealty, however informal, and Philemon had accepted enough in his time as Prince of Tasnim to know not to refuse. Gingerly, he took the knife and nodded.

It was a small blade to have taken the life of such a large man. Small and delicately curved, yet the blade was wickedly sharp. The hilt was worn from use, any sharp edges softened by the grip of how many hands? A dagger passed down through generations of desert people, until being buried in the guts of some insignificant sheikh. A dagger whose owner would surely return for such a valuable weapon.

Philemon looked up. The men were gone, leaving him alone with Anahita. He dropped the dagger where the bloodied carpet had once lay. It sliced into the sand and stood, hilt deep, as though it would murder the whole desert next.

Philemon shivered. He had to do something before the dagger's owner returned and tried to use it on Anahita, too.

"You're a fool, Philemon the frog," Anahita said, rising to her feet. "You should have stayed out of this."

Philemon seized her shoulders. "How could I? The whole camp could talk of nothing but how they would kill you and your husband on your wedding night. He could have killed you! And he'll be back, once he realises he left his knife behind. What in heaven's name made you blame his death on me? The real killer is out there, and it's only a matter of time before he claims leadership over this squalid camp for killing the last leader. What do you think he'll do to me for trying to claim his kill? Or you?"

Anahita tossed her head and met his eyes. "What else was I to do? They should have taken you into custody, and the moment you left this excuse for a boudoir – " she kicked one of the cushions that the men had missed " – the moment you left, you'd turn back into a frog, and escape. In the chaos that ensued, my men and I would be able to escape unseen. By the time they remembered us, we would be well on our way!" Her eyes narrowed. "Now, take your hands off me, or I will turn you into a eunuch like Haidar and Asad."

The shiver of steel touched his groin.

"Do your bits grow back when you turn back into a frog?" she asked.

Philemon released her, stumbling back. His eyes went to the knife, but it had vanished from the sand, as if it had never been.

She twisted the silky belt slung across her hips, and sheathed the knife. Another twist and the belt was back in place, an innocuous-seeming string of bells that hid a deadly secret.

"You killed him," Philemon whispered, not wanting to believe it. "What did he ever do to you?"

Anahita shrugged, a smile twisting her lips. "Nothing. I saw to that. That disgusting old man will never steal another woman from her husband again, or attack my father's people. On the morrow, or the next day, my men will find an excuse to slip away with me, and we will return home. I am a woman of my word — you may come home with us. But no one can ever know what I did here tonight. Or I will use one of my blades on you."

Philemon choked. "One of your blades? You have more?" He stared at her. She wore little more than the belt, and smaller versions of it at her wrists and ankles. Why, she was practically naked! Philemon averted his eyes. "How many more?" he asked, trying not the think of her smooth, curved flesh.

"Seven," she said. "Seven more."

He stared at her in horror. Her face, not the rest of her. "Seven?" His mouth was suddenly dry. For all he'd travelled with her, he barely knew this barbarian princess. He should have listened to her. Should have stayed in the waterskin, just like she'd said. Then he wouldn't know any of this, and he'd be blissfully ignorant that the woman he'd fallen in love with was some sort of demon. "Of course. Forgive me for worrying about your safety. You can take care of yourself, I see now." He turned on his heel and headed for the exit.

"Please don't go."

His foot hovered above the sand — sand that should be saturated with her bridegroom's blood — but Philemon hesitated to put it down on what was, to him, another man's grave. A man he had wished gone only hours before.

"I'm only doing what you asked me to. Returning to where I belong, to wait until we leave."

"Wait until morning. Please. It's my wedding night. I should not be alone." There was an edge of desperation in her voice – or did he imagine it?

"Then perhaps you should not have killed your husband. He could have warmed your bed. I…cannot." Because, heaven help him, he wanted her. Never mind the knives or that she'd killed a man or pinned the crime on him. If he shared her bed tonight, he wouldn't be able to keep his hands off her.

She lifted her chin. "I had no choice. Do you think I like killing? My first husband deserved his fate, a dozen times over, but I had no grudge against this one until today. But I swore an oath, and my father heard me do it. So he sends me to be his assassin, in the name of peace. He keeps his hands clean, yet mine are awash in blood. As always, on my wedding night. Such is my fate."

"It is not the fate you deserve. If you were my bride, your wedding night would be glorious, as it should be. I swear it."

She stared at him — it was her turn to be shocked.

Philemon wished he hadn't said it. To admit his weakness in front of her…why, she could stab him in the heart without needing any of her seven blades.

"Normally, my men would take me away — the hysterical bride — to calm me down, and when the nightmares invade my sleep, we are too far from the camp for anyone to hear my screams. But tonight you were here, and you made me stay. Why are you here, Philemon?"

She hadn't called him a frog. He took it as encouragement, however tiny it might be. "Because I couldn't let them kill you with him. Even let you witness what they intended to do to him. You deserve better. A wedding night to remember, for the right reasons, not the wrong ones."

She laughed softly. "I remember all my wedding nights, especially the first. I've survived five husbands, and five wedding nights I would give anything to forget."

"Let me make it up to you. Tonight." The moment the words left his lips, he regretted them. And yet…now they were out, he had nothing left to lose. "Give me one night, I beg you. From now until dawn. I will finish what we started last night with that exquisite kiss. If I cannot deliver what I promise – a wedding night like you deserve, filled with the pleasure such a lovely princess deserves – then do what you will with me. Carve me up and feed me to your falcon." He spread his arms wide and closed his eyes.

Thirty-Three

Faced with Philemon in all his naked glory, completely at her mercy…for the first time, Anahita felt shy.

She unfastened the cuffs at her wrists, letting them tinkle to the floor, followed by her belt, and finally the ankle cuffs. Naked and unarmed, her breathing short and ragged, she crossed the cushions until she stood before him.

Anahita took a deep breath, then took his face in her hands. She stretched up even as he yielded to her, and their lips met. Even before her lips parted, he stole her breath, so tender was his kiss. She could kiss him all night.

And yet…her heels dropped to the floor, so she looked up at him longingly. "I'm afraid," she whispered.

Her traitorous body reminded her what showing fear had done in the past – her body, flying through the air, from the force of her husband's blow. The explosion of pain, the fear of more, her voice silenced, her vision dulled…

Philemon's arms enfolded her. "You have nothing to fear from me. I promise. Tell me what you wish for, and I shall grant it. Your own personal djinn."

She managed a smile. "Then can we kiss a little more? And then…can I sleep in your arms?"

He lifted her in his arms, effortlessly. "As you wish, Princess."

Thirty-Four

"Do you know how to pleasure a woman?"

With Anahita naked in his arms, Philemon struggled vainly to think of anything but what he wanted to do to her. Her words made him lose the battle.

"Oh, yes. In many different ways," he began, wondering if he dared hope.

"With your fingers?" Anahita asked.

Ah, he'd forgotten she was a new bride on her as-yet unconsummated wedding night. A bride who had never known a man's touch.

He considered for a moment, before he

decided to take the risk. "Would you like me to show you?"

"Yes," she said promptly.

In the silence that followed his loss for words, she continued, "When I can't sleep and the dreams return, it's the only way to distract my mind from the memories. If I'm asking too much, Philemon, merely say so, and I will…I will attempt to take care of myself."

His imagination ran riot at the thought of her pleasuring herself in his arms, but the selfish part of him shut down that particular idea. She'd asked him for pleasure, and he intended to give it to her.

"You tell me if it is too much," he whispered, skimming his hand over her hip and between her thighs. She gave a little sigh, parting her legs wider, as his fingers found the right spot.

Philemon wrapped his other arm around her chest and pulled her firmly against him, revelling in the increasing tempo of her heartbeat as his fingers worked the only magic he knew.

Anahita began to moan softly, squirming in

his grasp to drive his fingers deeper inside her. She ground her soft little arse against his groin, turning him hard as a rock. He'd give anything to slip more than his fingers inside her. Just one thrust…

She bucked, arching her back away from him as she cried out, not once but twice, trapping his hand between her tightly clenched thighs.

When the moment ended and she lay limp and panting in his arms, Anahita whispered, "I've never…it's never felt that good before. Not even when Haidar – "

"I'm a man, not a eunuch," Philemon snapped, fighting the jealousy curling up at the mention of the eunuch's name. How could she think of any other man when she lay, sated, in his arms?

"I know." She reached down and cupped him, and he was proud to realise it took both of her hands to do it.

It took all of his self-control not to thrust into her warm hands, and demand that she reciprocate. The bliss of those soft hands stroking him, or those wicked lips wrapped around him…

"Do you know how to pleasure a woman with this?"

Philemon grinned. Oh, she was a maiden, all right. No woman who'd ever been loved by a man would have to ask such a question. "A hundred…nay…a thousand times better than with my hands," he assured her. He wanted to beg her to let him show her, but he knew that was too much to ask.

She squirmed around so that she faced him, her oasis eyes fathomless pools in the darkness. "If you can, I give you my word that you may share my bed every night until I return home."

His breath caught in his throat. Was she really asking…?

Anahita took his hesitation for reluctance. "And when we reach home, I will press my sister into finding the enchantress who cursed you, and making her break the curse. If you show me the pleasure you would show your bride on her wedding night." She moistened her lips. "Please."

He reached up to cup her face in his hands.

"On a wedding night, the pleasure must be shared," he said, then kissed her.

She stiffened at first – kissing was still too new to her – before Anahita melted into his touch, kissing him back with far more passion than he'd hoped for.

Thirty-Five

Philemon entered her slowly, as though terrified he would break her if he thrust too hard or fast.

"We only have until dawn," Anahita said, feeling it would be churlish to tell him to hurry up.

He swallowed. "I don't want to hurt you, and as this is your first time…"

She couldn't help it. She laughed. "My first time? Truly, you thought that? My first time, the bastard beat me so badly my eyes were nearly swelled shut, then cracked my head against the tent pole so I could not see him nor fight back when he raped me. I deserved the pain, for tempting him so wickedly with my body, or so he said. I learned later his man parts wouldn't work unless the woman he wanted was cowering in fear. I only wish he'd died more slowly than he did, for I know he deserved more pain than he ever put me through." She sobered. "I was widowed for the fifth time tonight, but I will never let a man hurt me again."

"And if I fail to please you, you'll make me the sixth man to die at your feet?"

"Hardly. You are not my husband. My father does not want you dead, and neither do I. You are a most agreeable travelling companion. Perhaps even more than that if you show me the pleasure you promised tonight." More pleasure than he had already.

He nodded. "Very well." And in one smooth motion, he filled her completely.

She took a deep breath, relishing the heat of him inside her, touching exactly where his fingers had stroked her to ecstasy not long before. Truly, she wanted this. Wanted him.

She didn't even need to say it. He looked into her eyes, and saw it all, from that very first thrust until he pushed her all the way to an incredible peak where they cried out for joy together.

And as he folded her into his arms afterwards, she pressed her ear to his chest, to hear his still-racing heart, beating in rhythm with hers. "Will you love me like that again tomorrow night?" she asked sleepily.

"Every night. I'll love you like that every night you desire," Philemon said.

"Mmmm. You should not say such things, you know, for after tonight, I will desire you every night, as long as I live." She smiled. "My prince."

"It will be my pleasure, Princess."

Thirty-Six

Philemon awoke to the sweet smell of the soft girl in his arms, and for a moment, he wondered whether he had died in his sleep and flown direct to heaven. But Anahita was no houri. She was a living, breathing woman he would do anything to keep.

A woman who deserved a proper husband, not one who would turn back into a frog when the sun rose. And she did not deserve to wake up beside his slimy self today, after the pleasures of last night. He should leave now, and return to his hiding place among the water skins to await their journey home.

He must have jostled her, for her hand shot out and grabbed his arm. "Don't go." Her oasis eyes reproached him.

"It is nearly dawn, and you know what happens then," he said, pulling away.

"Make love to me once more. There is still time," she said.

Philemon shook his head. "Lovemaking should not be rushed. I will turn back into a frog before we are finished, and you will throw me out of your bed in disgust."

"Never," she declared, creeping closer. He tried not to moan as her hand wrapped around his length. "You were thinking of it, too. Love me like you want to."

Despite his misgivings, he could not refuse her. And once their bodies joined, he was lost to anything but her pleasure, and his own.

Until she lay on the cushions, sated, her breasts heaving as she recovered from the exertion. Oh, how he loved her.

"Honoured Sheikh, I bring food and water, so that you may wash and break your fast. The women are waiting to tend to your wife, too, when you are finished with her." Philemon recognised the man who'd handed him the knife last night, before he bowed deeply and hid his face.

Philemon tugged a cloth up over Anahita's breasts, chagrined at the need to hide them from view. "I will never be finished with her," he said honestly.

Anahita gasped, but the man didn't seem to hear, for he ducked his head and said, "I understand, Honoured Sheikh, but the men of the camp need your leadership. With Basit gone, they look to you, and it is nearly noon. The women…they, too, need to know your orders. Basit beat them if they did not deliver the dinner he desired, and they do not wish to displease you."

Noon. How was he still human, if it was noon?

His met Anahita's wide eyes – she recognised the significance, even if she understood it no better than he did.

"My wife will instruct them," he said, his eyes begging her to agree.

A secretive smile twisted Anahita's lips

before she ducked her head to hide it. "As my prince commands."

Then the tent was full of women, helping Anahita wash and dress.

Philemon rose, clutching a sheet to cover his modesty.

One of the women bowed deeply. "For you, Honoured Sheikh." She held out what appeared to be fresh robes.

Oh, heavens be praised. He snatched them from her. He'd never dressed so quickly in his life. Yet as he reached the entrance of his tent, he hesitated. He had not stood in the sun in his own form for too long. Would the curse turn him green again once the sunlight touched him?

Only one way to find out. Philemon stepped out into the sunlight, glad of his sandals as the very air seemed to want to sear his skin off.

"Honoured Sheikh?" The knife man stood uncertainly at his side.

Enough of this sheikh business. "It's Highness, actually. I'm Prince Philemon of Tasnim." Oh, it felt good to say it. Not as good as he'd felt twined around Anahita in the throes of passion, but it was a distant second.

The man fell to his knees and touched his forehead to the burning sand. "Oh, please forgive me, Your Highness. I did not know!"

He'd burn his face off if he stayed down there, Philemon knew. He seized the man's shoulder and hauled him to his feet. "Of course you didn't, because I didn't tell you until now. What is your name?"

"Tariq, Highness," the man said, not daring to raise his eyes to Philemon's face.

"So, yesterday, who would you have expected to succeed Basit as sheikh?" Philemon asked.

"I don't understand, Your Highness," Tariq said cautiously.

"Yesterday, your people couldn't wait to get rid of him. Who did you think would take his place?" Philemon asked, watching Tariq's face carefully.

Tariq hesitated, them said, "Why, the strongest among us, the best leader, like yourself, Your Highness."

Now Philemon wished he had been the one to kill Basit. A right fearmongering bastard.

"I'm not staying, Tariq. I must return to Tasnim. I didn't leave the richest city in the world to come and lead a desert tribe. I'm not your new sheikh. Your people must choose their own leader." Philemon heard the man splutter behind him, but he no longer needed a guide – the tent where they'd held the wedding feast the previous day hummed with the sound of men's voices. Waiting for him.

He marched in, calling for quiet.

Philemon had to hide a smile when Tariq's voice rose to a roar, drowning out all other sound: "Bow before His Royal Highness, Prince Philemon of Tasnim!"

No bowing happened, but Philemon did get stunned silence. It was enough.

He explained the things he'd told Tariq, and how he would be returning home as soon as possible.

"And what about our wives?" one man shouted. "Are you taking them, too?" Half a dozen others took up the same cry.

Philemon sighed inwardly. He had no desire to lead any part of a desert tribe – or steal its women. "The only woman who will leave with me is the Sultan's daughter, Princess Anahita."

A collective sigh of relief went up from the assembled men.

"Where is she?" a familiar voice demanded.

Philemon scanned the crowd and found them at the back – Anahita's men. They did not look relieved.

"In the women's tent, I believe, seeing to our midday meal," Philemon said airily, as if it mattered little to him. Ha. His thoughts were with her every moment they were apart, though he knew she was in no danger with a pack of cowed women.

"She'd better not be cooking it herself, or she'll poison us all. I've seen the princess burn water," the man – Asad? – shouted back.

Nervous laughter erupted around him.

Philemon cast his mind back. All those nights he'd travelled with them…had Anahita ever cooked anything? He couldn't recall her preparing any food, except occasionally skinning whatever that devilish bird of hers caught. He should have noticed her skill with a blade before. Too late now.

Philemon mumbled something about

making sure, and out of the tent toward the one where the women resided.

A boy stood at the door. A guard, perhaps? His eyes widened when he saw Philemon, and his mouth dropped open, no sound coming out.

Philemon nodded and stepped into the dimly lit space.

"The new Sheikh! The new Sheikh is here!" The boy had regained the use of his voice.

Philemon held up his hands in surrender. He knew better than to invade the domain of women without explaining himself first. "I seek Princess Anahita."

"You could have waited until I'd finished bathing, and I'd had something to break my fast," she grumbled as her head emerged from a tunic as heavily embroidered as the last two she'd worn. "After last night, I'm sure you don't need me again already."

He couldn't help it. Just the sight of her brought a smile to his lips. How had he ever lived without her? "I will always need you."

She narrowed her eyes. "And what about all your concubines, hmm?"

"I have none, and never will again. The only woman I will ever need now is you." Philemon wet his lips. "I will see you crowned as the Princess of Tasnim, if you wish it."

Anahita spread her arms wide. "And what of the other women here? Basit made them all his concubines. They were wives, daughters, all stolen from their families. What will you do with them, Sheikh?" She spat the title like the worst epithet.

Philemon shook his head. "I am no sheikh. I am Prince Philemon of Tasnim, and I declare you are free to return to your families as honourable widows, with all that entails. Any man who says otherwise will answer to me."

Only now did he realise all eyes were upon him. "I told the guards this last night. Didn't they pass the message on?"

Anahita's fingers laced through his. "I said the same thing, but no one believed me. See? I told you he is not a monster." She stared up at him, and for a moment he thought she would kiss him. Then her gaze darted down. "Except when he keeps me too busy for breakfast. I'm sure there is a law against denying a new bride her breakfast!"

A woman Philemon didn't know laid a hand on Anahita's shoulder. "Take the prince to one of the common tents. Congratulations to you both. I will bring a wedding breakfast for you."

Thirty-Seven

In between bites of food and congratulations from what seemed like every man and woman in the camp at becoming their new sheikh, Anahita tried to ask him how he'd managed to break the curse. Philemon heard the question, she was certain of it, but he was too busy thanking someone to answer it right away.

And then another interruption, and another, until she wanted to scream, if her throat still wasn't raw from last night.

Finally, the tide of humanity seemed to decide to give them a moment alone.

"How did you break the curse?" she demanded.

He shrugged. "I wish I knew. Perhaps it was you. I do not remember the witch's exact words when she first cursed me, but she definitely mentioned a princess's bed, and something about dusk or maybe dawn. If we find her, perhaps we can ask her. But in the meantime, I mean to enjoy being a man again. A man who will travel home with you, as soon as possible, if your word still holds true."

"It does," she said, stung. "But why do you need to travel with us now? As the Prince of Tasnim, and the sheikh of this place, surely you can command your people to come with you, or take you wherever you wish."

He leaned close so his breath tickled her ear. "I promised to take you to Tasnim, my home, and prove that I am its prince. The witch didn't just curse me — when she came, the water supply dried up, too. I must see it restored, even if it means hunting her down."

"I will help you," she said. Because if she could go to Tasnim…she could finally be free.

Philemon took her hand in his and kissed it.

"And I will be grateful for any further assistance you wish to offer, Princess. For after seeing you break one curse, I have no doubt you will save my city as you have me."

Anahita wasn't sure about that, but another group of people came up to offer their congratulations, so she held her tongue.

Thirty-Eight

Philemon would have given everything he owned to bypass the oasis without having to look at the accursed place, but his travel companions were having none of it. Besides, with the wells of Tasnim still dry, they would need to replenish their water supplies.

He busied himself helping the other men unload the camels and set up camp. A task for servants, but Anahita had made it clear there were no servants or masters in this travelling party. A peculiar princess indeed.

She stood at the water's edge, wearing a pair

of flimsy sandals and a short tunic. They might have been the same ones she'd worn the day they met. Then, she'd taken him in her hands, lifting him out of despondency and saving him from certain death. An irresistible desire rose up within him, to take her in his arms and never let her go.

His feet carried him across the sand of their own accord, and she yielded to his embrace as she yielded to no one else. He pressed his lips to the back of her neck, tasting the salt of sweat she'd said she wanted to wash off.

"Why do you hesitate?" he asked. Even he felt the pull of the cool water, which held no dread for him when he was with her. Anahita had broken the curse once – he was in no danger of being cursed again while he had her.

"The water is not as clear as before, and the level has risen." She pointed. "Those baby date palms were well away from the edge before, but now they are submerged. Merlin insists there are frogs here, too, where there were none but you last time we were here. And now the water is warm, which it wasn't the first time." She shook her head. "I don't know what that means."

He helped her out of her tunic, and hurried to remove his own clothes. "Then we should wash, and wait for your bird to catch a frog. Perhaps you can question the creature."

Anahita smiled. "I have enough cursed princes to last me a lifetime. And I have no intention of sharing my bed with any man but you."

He kissed her. "Good."

They took their time in the water, for washing soon led to other things, which meant more washing, before they emerged. Moonrise in the twilight sky shimmered across Anahita's damp skin, before she slipped on a robe to cover herself.

"Dinner's ready!" Asad called.

Philemon hurried to don his own clothes, before heading to the fire, where the other three had already taken their seats.

"There must have been some rain in the mountains. We'll have to watch out for the rivers, and be careful crossing them," Asad said.

Philemon laughed. "How can you possibly

know that? I haven't seen a single cloud in the sky!"

"The water here. It's been muddied by floodwaters, which only come when a deluge washes things down from the mountains. And the frogs, of course. That silly bird ate so many, she's too fat to fly any more." Asad pointed at Anahita's falcon, who did look rounder than usual. He snorted. "I hope none of them were your brothers, Philemon. She ate them while you two were taking your time in the water, and I don't speak frog."

Anahita's blush was barely visible in the firelight, but there was no hiding it from Philemon, or the other men who knew her so well. "None of them spoke. Not like Philemon when Merlin caught him. They were ordinary frogs. Proper frogs, according to Merlin." She rose and headed over to the bird.

Haidar tipped the dregs of his cup out onto the sand, then poured himself another drink. "You may please her now, enough for her to accept you as her husband, but one wrong step and there are plenty of places where a body can be buried in the sand and never seen again.

Don't forget that, Frog Prince."

For a moment, Philemon wondered what it would be like to fight the man. A fair fight in the training ring, of course. Haidar was a better fighter than Anahita, and he had size and strength on his side, too, but it would be a fine fight, while it lasted. One Anahita would never allow, he was certain of it.

Philemon lifted his cup in acknowledgement. "And should I die in the desert at the point of the princess's blade, I thank you for the courtesy of a proper burial. For we both know you wouldn't deny her the pleasure of cutting out my heart, if that is her desire."

Asad exploded into laughter. "It's your manhood she'll cut off, and you'll live just long enough to watch it burn. Falling in love with her is foolishness."

Haidar threw his cup down on the sand and stalked away, muttering to himself.

"Should you go after him?" Philemon asked.

Asad snorted. "No. You're both as foolish as each other, and he knows it. But that doesn't alter the fact that he'll enjoy watching you die if you've lied to the princess about being a prince, or Tasnim. The one thing he loves almost as much as the girl herself is defending her honour. So if any part of your story isn't true, now's the time to disappear. Just take care at the river crossings, or your body will be swept away as easily as the princess has swept away your senses."

"I have lied about nothing," Philemon declared. "Which is more than I can say about you. Who ever heard of storms in a clear sky? Where is all the water you say will cause a flood?"

Asad grinned, his eyes glittering in the firelight. "Not all the water in the desert is where we can see it. Deep beneath the surface, there are underground rivers and lakes. The same sort that lies beneath Tasnim, and provides it with so much of its water. It bubbles up in wadis and springs like this one, but this is a mere puddle compared to what lies below. And with so much more water here…it'll be a wonder if your cave city isn't completely flooded."

Philemon's heart constricted in his chest.

"Tasnim has never flooded. Never. The water is gone. It cannot flood!" For if the treasure chambers on the lowest levels flooded, he would be penniless. The Sultan would not let him marry Anahita then. He swallowed. "I will show you on the morrow. My city has survived for a thousand years, and it will survive a thousand more."

Asad's smile didn't fade as he turned to stare into the fire. "We shall see, Frog Prince. For a man who didn't know about the rivers beneath the desert a moment ago, you'll forgive me if I don't believe your expert assessment of them now."

Thirty-Nine

Philemon's frantic lovemaking last night spoke of some emotional disquiet he refused to tell her. Fear had his eyes darting everywhere, above a mouth that couldn't seem to smile, as they approached his home.

It was a strange transformation. All the way to Basit's camp, he'd entertained Anahita with tales of the beauties of Tasnim, but now he seemed terrified to show them to her.

Determined to solve this mystery before she arrived, Anahita urged her camel to match Philemon's pace. Her happy travel companion was now too busy scowling at the horizon to notice her.

"Tell me about your last day in Tasnim," she said.

He glanced up for only a moment before the horizon drew his gaze once more. "Is that an order?"

"We made a deal. You amuse me while we travel, and I take you home. Well, I don't find your silence amusing. I find it…alarming. And I want to know what I'm walking into. Sometimes knives are not enough. Especially if there is an enchantress who turns innocent princes into frogs." Anahita managed a smile. "I'm hardly innocent."

"She will not touch you. If she even attempts to cast a spell in your direction, I shall – " Philemon stopped, then continued, "I shall stand in her way, and force her to curse me instead. In the meantime, your men will use her distraction to…deal with her."

"And then I will have to break the curse again, though I don't know how I did it the first time? You place great faith in me. Faith I don't share. Tell me what happened. What are we walking into that has you so scared?" Anahita pressed.

Philemon sighed deeply and buried his head in his hands. "There is nothing in Tasnim that will harm you. Not even her. I am not innocent, either. I fear…I fear I may have deserved the curse, and if there is anyone in Tasnim, they will blame me for the fall of the city, too."

Anahita persisted. "But you can't possibly be responsible for the wells running dry. It would take a powerful curse, or spell or…"

"It was a wish, granted by a particularly powerful djinn, actually. A careless wish that once granted, could not be undone." Now Philemon refused to meet her eyes at all.

But Anahita would not be diverted from her course. "What did you wish for?"

He let out a harsh laugh. "What does any man wish for in the desert? An oasis, where he might drink and refresh himself." When Anahita didn't respond, he went on: "The oasis where you found me, actually. A place where you could not resist bathing, either."

And the tale came spilling out, at first in

spurts and starts, before finally it gushed out of Philemon, a flow of words that could not be stopped.

A djinn who obeyed orders without question, creating an oasis for his master without caring about the consequences.

A city slowly starved of water until the wells ran dry.

A prince who demanded the oh-so-powerful djinn fix the problem, only to be told it required more power than the djinn possessed to refill the underwater reservoir.

A call for help, the help of a powerful enchantress who did have the power to compel the djinn to obey.

An enchantress who imprisoned the djinn, but who could not return the water to his home.

A fool of a prince who threw the enchantress out of the city, unthanked and unpaid, for she had not restored his city's water supply.

A city of people, trying to leave, and an enraged enchantress who could not be kept out.

An enchantress who cast him into a well, then led the evacuation herself, saving his people.

A fool of a prince, turned frog, hopping from puddle to puddle as he chased what remained of his city's water supply...all the way down to the new oasis, where he finally understood: no magic in the world was powerful enough to make water run uphill. Or to change the past.

"But it's not your fault," Anahita said slowly.

"It is," Philemon insisted. "I made that foolish wish, and I am the city's prince. The responsibility is mine. I know that now."

"But the djinn. He should have said something..."

Philemon shook his head. "You don't know djinn. They are slaves, bound by magic to obey their masters, without question. The only time they can refuse is if they are not powerful enough to grant their master's wish. Something I realised too late. I made the wish, so the responsibility for it is mine. Tasnim was a city of wonders, and she died of thirst in the desert because of me."

"Then what are you afraid of?" Anahita still didn't understand.

Philemon reached out and grabbed her hand. Her startled eyes met his – and an intensity she could not look away from.

"Have you ever killed a man who didn't deserve it?" he demanded.

"Of course not. All of them were bastards. Men who killed innocent men and women, not caring who they destroyed as they pursued their desires. They deserved far worse than I gave them, I promise you." Anahita tried to pull her hand back, but he held it fast.

"What do you think I did to Tasnim? I destroyed a city to grant the most insignificant desire. How am I any better than the rest of them? You should have killed me then, but you'll definitely do it when you see the ghost my beautiful city has become."

He released her and urged his camel into a gallop, putting space between them Anahita had no way to close.

It was for the best. Few people had seen Anahita cry, and if the desert drank her tears, no one would ever know how her heart wept for Philemon and all he had lost.

Because he was wrong. He was nothing like Fakhri or Basit or any of the others. None of them had ever showed a moment of remorse for their actions, or even regret.

And as the tears dried on her cheeks in the searing desert heat, she made a new vow. Men might die, but a city's life was in her people. If she could help Philemon return Tasnim to its former glory, then she would do everything in her power to make that happen. Because to turn Philemon the frog into the true prince he deserved to be, he needed his domain back. His home.

Forty

Philemon touched the stone that marked the gates of Tasnim. Twenty men could not move it, but when he laid his hand on it, it rolled aside as though it weighed nothing. Part of the enchantments the door guardian had laid on the place, in the centuries he had watched over the city.

The silence struck him first. The city should be bustling, but it was empty. Of people, of movement, of life. He had done this.

Perhaps he should not show this to Anahita now. He wanted her to see the city at its best, not the empty shell of what it once was.

But without her help…how could he ever bring it back to life?

Reluctantly, he led the way inside.

Anahita's fingers found his, lacing them together as she stood at his side. "So this is the legendary city of Tasnim. It looks like a sandstorm came through, and the people are just waiting for it to be safe before they sweep the sand away."

Sand, not water. Asad's predictions of flooding had not come to pass. He breathed a sigh of relief, but it was short lived. For the sand was deeper than he'd ever seen it.

More than one sandstorm had done this. The air vents and light wells couldn't keep the desert out for long, but it was piled up in drifts against the walls, leaving swathes of stone floor clear to walk across. How long had he been gone?

There was no way of telling down here. Unlike the sand, time had stood still.

He led the way to the well by which he'd last left the city. A quick peek into the houses along the way revealed…little. They'd been left as if their owners had simply gone on a journey, and intended to return. The beds were made up, ready for their owners' return, and some kitchens still had bags and casks of food in them, waiting to be opened for the next meal.

The well hadn't changed a bit. He must have already been a frog when he fell in, Philemon decided. He knelt down beside the low stone wall that normally kept people from falling in, and scrabbled around in the sand. He unearthed a robe. When he shook the sand out of it, he recognised it as the one he'd been wearing that fateful day. If his clothes were here, then his ring of office must be, too – and the door guardian djinn.

Desperately, he sifted through the sand, searching, but no ring emerged. He'd come back later and search, he promised himself.

"Didn't you say the water is all gone?" Anahita asked.

"Yes," Philemon admitted. "We will find a way to bring it back." If such a thing was possible.

"But I can hear it," she insisted. She knelt,

took a pebble from the floor, and threw it into the well. They both heard it plop into water that sounded too deep to be true.

With shaking hands, Philemon lowered his torch as far as he could without falling in. Again. Light gleamed on the water, not far below.

"It's real. It's returned!" he blurted out. He dropped his torch on the ground, wrapped both arms around her, and kissed her. "You did it. I don't know how, but you did!" He kissed her again, and again. He never wanted to stop.

"I didn't do anything!' she protested. "And the water might be back, but where are your people? Do they know the waters have returned?"

He reluctantly turned his mind to more mundane matters. "No, they must not. I must go to the capital and find criers willing to shout it from the rooftops that Tasnim citizens can come home."

"The capital." She did not sound so eager to go home as he thought she'd been.

"Of course. We must also buy provisions,

for I am sure the people took what they could when they left."

This didn't lift her frown at all.

"Would you like to see the fabled jewelled gardens of Tasnim? Words cannot describe their beauty – you must see them with your own eyes to fully appreciate them."

A small smile graced her lips. "I've heard so much about them."

Taking her hand, he led the way to the harem gardens, wishing with all his heart that he would find a way to make this her home.

He stepped into the hall that held the most wondrous trees known to man, lifting his torch so that she might see them better. And stopped.

"What bastard stole my garden?" Philemon roared.

Forty-One

It took time to calm Philemon down and persuade him that the capital was probably the best place to start looking for the thief, though Anahita suspected that the jewels and precious metals had most likely been melted down and made into smaller, more portable things by now.

Nevertheless, he agreed, and within two days, they'd reached the capital. A city that changed little, usually.

"That went up quickly. I didn't know Father intended to build a new palace, and we haven't been gone that long. Do you remember hearing anything about this…edifice?" Anahita asked, peering through the gleaming gates of the brand new palace.

Haidar shrugged. "Nothing at all. Palaces take years to build, not weeks. I smell magic at work."

Magic that could erect a palace in a matter of weeks was potent stuff indeed. Whoever had built this place was more powerful than anyone Anahita had ever met.

Haidar exchanged a few words with the guard, then returned to Anahita's side, his frown deeper than ever. "He said this palace belongs to the Prince of Tasnim and his wife, Princess Maram."

Anahita's mouth dropped open beneath her veil. "Maram will never marry, and the Prince of Tasnim is…" She waved at Philemon.

"Not about to tolerate imposters," Philemon said softly, marching toward the gate with murder in his eyes.

"No, wait," Anahita said. "If Maram has truly married the man, she would never refuse to see me. Or the men with me, for she knows

I am never without Haidar and Asad." She turned to Haidar. "Tell him who I am, and that I wish to seek consolation for my bereavement with my sister."

Haidar bowed low, hiding his grin. "As Your Highness wishes."

While they waited for a guard to find out if Maram was willing to see her sister, Anahita lowered her voice to share her plan. "Haidar, Asad, return to the palace, and see that my things are taken where they belong. Have the servants prepare an evening meal for me, for I will be home then. Philemon can accompany me as my guard – " she laid a hand on his arm, shooting him a meaningful glance " – until we know more. When the time is right, then reveal yourself, and lay the imposter bare."

Philemon inclined his head. "Spoken like a true assassin."

Anahita hushed him, scanning the people around to see if anyone had heard. Thankfully, no one appeared to have been listening.

The gates swung open and both guards bowed. "Princess Maram welcomes Princess Anahita to her home."

Anahita recognised the maid who met them at the door. "Yasmeen? So Maram really is here?"

Yasmeen bowed. "Yes, Princess. This palace was a gift to Her Highness from her new husband. He even built her a bathhouse so that she might not need to cross the city to use the one by the gates. She still does, of course, but not every day now." She giggled. "Her Highness does not like to leave her husband."

"So Maram is…happy to be married?" Anahita ventured.

"I have never seen Her Highness happier." Yasmeen's tone was rich with satisfaction. She definitely approved of Maram's marriage.

"And what of her husband?"

"The Master is most kind."

Master. An interesting title, for a man who styled himself as a prince. Whoever he was, he was wealthier than her own father, for this palace was grander inside than out. Quite a feat. His wealth must have been what swayed the Sultan to let Maram marry. But it would not have won over Maram.

And, unlike most other women in the

harem, Maram would not have confided her secrets to her maid.

So Anahita followed Yasmeen in silence, admiring the mosaics that rose from the floor to cover the walls and the ceiling. Whoever he was, he had an eye for detail and beauty, to command such work for Maram. Perhaps he truly loved her.

What man wouldn't?

Philemon's footsteps echoed angrily behind her, more stomps than steps. A quick glance back told her he had noticed the wealth they walked within, and it only inflamed his temper further. A man who could build such a place had no need to pretend to be a prince. He could have bought himself a small kingdom somewhere with the price he'd have paid for this palace alone.

Then why…?

Maram rose to greet them, her hair flowing like a dark river over her shoulders and her cerise silk gown. "What are you still wearing your veil for?" Maram chided, reaching for Anahita's face.

"Your husband…I thought…" Anahita

stammered.

Maram clucked her tongue. "No need to worry about him. You are among family here."

A hand seized Maram's wrist before she could touch Anahita. "No one touches Princess Anahita without the princess's permission," Philemon rumbled warningly.

Maram's eyes flared blue as the turned her gaze on Philemon. "But to touch Princess Maram is to lose your heart and mind in love for her, for you are not one of her usual men. Are you?" She lifted her captured wrist and spun in his grasp, a graceful dancer's twirl that highlighted her perfect figure as the silk swirled around her.

"Is he why you won't uncover your face, Ana? For he's no eunuch – see?" Maram pointed.

Philemon released Maram and seized Anahita instead, pulling her body against his to shield her from…Maram? Now Anahita couldn't help but notice his arousal, for it grew harder still with the close contact.

"Stand back, witch! Your foul spell will not work on me. I love only one woman, and no witch will tear her from me!" Philemon ripped his sword from its scabbard and pointed it at Maram. "Back, I said!"

After the enchantress who'd cursed him, he could see no good in any magic wielder. He would cut her down, he feared her magic that much.

No. This couldn't happen. Not Maram.

Her blades were in her hands before Anahita had time to think. One at Philemon's throat, while a second aimed for a lower target.

"Drop your sword, or you'll lose the other one," Anahita said. Tears welled up, but she stood firm. No matter how much she loved him, she would not let Philemon hurt her sister.

"Ana…" His eyes widened with betrayal.

"I swore an oath. Hurt her, and you are no better than Basit. And you shall share his fate." She begged him with her eyes. "Drop your sword."

Forty-Two

Philemon could not refuse her. He let the blade clatter to the floor.

Anahita kicked it out of reach. "Get out."

He stared at her. Surely she couldn't mean that.

"Is there anything you wish of me, my princess?" a new voice asked.

He stood in the doorway to the courtyard, too well-dressed to be a servant, yet not proud enough to be a prince. This lean man reminded him of a desert hunting falcon – tamed and kept hungry to serve one of the desert camps, waiting for his mistress's command.

The witch favoured him with a beaming smile. "My sister's man needs some air. Perhaps you could take him into the garden? He might find it cooler under the trees."

The man returned her smile, and bowed deeply. Not like a servant. More like…he was mocking her. He was the witch's lover, Philemon realised. "As you wish, Princess." He turned to the side and gestured toward Philemon. "Please, be my guest."

Philemon risked a glance back at Anahita, but her eyes still blazed with fury. She hadn't sheathed her knives.

Philemon sighed. "Very well." He followed the witch's lover.

"Men who threaten Maram tend to die gruesome deaths. You are the first she has ever invited to see her garden," the man said over his shoulder. "Perhaps it is because you are a man of the desert. The laws of hospitality are strong in the camps, or so I am told. She must be curious to discover what would make a man forget something so fundamental."

Philemon glanced down at his clothes, for

the first time realising what he must look like. He was dressed like a desert sheikh – had they mistaken him for Anahita's dead husband?

"I am not what I appear. I am, in fact, a man of Tasnim," Philemon said.

The witch's lover nodded slowly. "A city known for the high price of its hospitality." A faint smile touched his lips.

"Have you been there?" Philemon demanded.

"Once. I have no desire to return. It is a desolate place." The witch's lover dismissed it with a shrug of his shoulder.

Philemon bristled. "Now the waters have returned, so will its people. Tasnim will live again. I swear it."

"Spoken like a man who loves his home, and knows it is only home because of the people in it. I almost lost everything before I came to realise that. Without Maram, I am nothing." Another shrug, as though this man didn't care that his happiness depended on a woman – and a witch, at that.

"No man is nothing. Return with me to Tasnim, and I will show you that no man is worthless," Philemon said.

The man looked amused. "You would turn me into a man of Tasnim?"

Philemon opened his mouth to correct him, for the right to live in Tasnim was earned, not granted, except in the most unusual circumstances. Like saving the life of the prince, or some other such act of courage and service.

"Behold, the princess's garden." The man turned to the side, to let Philemon precede him. "Have you ever seen anything so wondrous?"

Philemon stepped from darkness into light – and what a wondrous light it was. Fractured rainbows, blinding, glittering, from every angle, both above and below. He shaded his eyes, squinting to find the source of so much light. The noon sun gazed down from above, but there was more to it. It was like standing in a cage of mirrors, or...

Philemon's heart turned to a burning lump of lead in his chest, firing his blood to boiling. "These are the jewelled gardens from the harem of Tasnim. Your Master stole these from me! Tell me his name, and I will grant you full citizenship of my city. He will die for this!" He reached for his sword, but the scabbard was empty. Too late, he realised he'd left the blade behind at Anahita's command, when he needed it now. "You stole these. You visited my city. How?"

A blue cloud erupted between Philemon and the witch's lover. "My Master is no thief, Philemon. I took them as my due, a price for service, as it were. And I was right to do so. Their splendour in sunlight is unmatched. You left them to be buried in dust and blown sand. My greatest creation!" The djinn door guardian spat on the floor at Philemon's feet. "You did not deserve them."

"Kaveh, that is no way to treat a guest in my house," the man chided.

"He means you harm – he threatened your life, just as he drew his sword on the princess!" the djinn insisted.

Realisation dawned on Philemon. "You're not the witch's lover. She's your wife – you're the man who was not content to just pretend to be a prince! My name, my garden…my door guardian! What else have you stolen from me?"

The man pulled a ring off his finger – a ring Philemon recognised. "I did not – "

"No!" the djinn howled, shoving the ring back on his master's finger. "You swore an oath. That ring is not to leave your finger until you pass it to your son on your deathbed!"

A djinn fighting his master? Philemon would not have believed such a thing was possible, if he hadn't seen it with his own eyes.

Philemon held out his hand. "That is my ring of office. I demand you hand it over, along with mastery of that disobedient djinn."

The djinn glared back at him. "You cast the ring aside, along with everyone else in the city, when you deserted us. Fadi sold that ring to a silversmith, so that he would have the money to feed your people. An evil wizard bought it, and gave it to Aladdin. It belongs to him and you shall not have it!"

Philemon ignored him. The fake prince was the key, he knew it. What had the djinn said his name was? "Aladdin, give me my ring, or I will tell your wife who is the real Prince of Tasnim. Let's see if Princess Maram wishes to be your wife when she knows the truth!"

"Please, enlighten me," a female voice purred.

The witch.

Philemon reached for his dagger.

"Oh, don't bother," she said. "She's gone home to her apartments in the Sultan's palace, and you've made your preferences perfectly clear. You fancy my sister, and against her better judgement and my own, she's still partial to you. She's never taken a lover before. She's more likely to take a man's life, than take him to bed. You must have been quite persuasive, Prince Philemon of Tasnim."

Philemon sagged. "Not persuasive enough, if she has left me."

Aladdin had the right of it. The world was empty without the woman he loved. He stared at the fake prince with sympathy, for the first time. The djinn had vanished.

"Perhaps not." The witch wet her lips. "Would you care for a wager, Philemon?"

"What do you have that I want?"

The witch smiled. "By the sound of things, everything. Your garden. Your title. Your symbol of office. And the woman you wish to be your wife."

She had him. "What do I have that you want?" Philemon asked, his heart sinking. He was back to promising all the wealth of Tasnim to a witch. If she turned him into a frog again…Anahita would not save him this time, he was sure of it.

"The power to make my dearest sister happy," she said. Her eyes filled with tears. "I would gamble my garden for that."

Philemon drew closer. "What do you mean?"

Maram waved her hand and a servant appeared. "Bring us refreshments. We have business to discuss." The maid scurried away.

Maram gazed into Philemon's eyes. A frank assessment of his soul, without a hint of the seduction she'd tried earlier. "You will go speak to the Sultan, and you will tell them Aladdin is your younger half-brother. And then you will tell him that seeing your brother's happiness, you must be married to another of my sisters at once."

Philemon shook his head. "Anahita will

never agree to it. You didn't see the way she looked at me."

Maram wet her lips. "That is where the wager comes in. If this works, she will be your wife, and I keep my garden. If this does not work…I will ask my husband to have another garden crafted for you to replace this one. Do we have a deal?"

Hope danced before Philemon, like Anahita on her wedding night. Tantalising, but too far away to touch. "And if she decides she wants me dead instead?"

Maram laughed. "If my sister wanted you dead, you'd be lying in a pool of your own blood in my reception room. Anahita does not hesitate…or she didn't, before you."

Could he gamble everything for love?

He stared at Aladdin, the pretend prince, who only had eyes for Maram. Her dark eyes were firmly fixed on Philemon.

"Yes," Philemon said. "Yes, we have a deal."

Forty-Three

The moment the men vanished, Maram tore the veil from Anahita's head. "Where did he hurt you?" she demanded, examining Anahita's face.

Anahita shook her head. "He didn't. Philemon has been everything I ever dreamed of until he threatened you."

"That's not Sheikh Basit?" Maram asked.

"No. Basit was old, fat, boring, and a bastard. He's also dead and buried. Philemon even tried to take the blame. Basit's people believed him." Because no one believed a woman was capable of defending herself, or killing a dangerous man. Least of all the men who'd died at her hands.

"So who is he, and where did you find him?" Maram asked.

The Prince of Tasnim, as a frog perched atop her hawk's head, soaring and screaming above an oasis. Anahita shook her head. "You won't believe me."

Maram smiled. "Would you believe I married a humble spinner's son, a man so poor he could scarcely afford to eat, who wandered into the wrong bathhouse?"

Anahita's mouth dropped open. "You mean…you married your lover from the bathhouse? I thought he was supposed to be a prince!"

Maram pressed a finger to her lips. "Father thinks so, which is why he agreed to the marriage. The palace helped, though."

"How did a man who couldn't afford food pay for this palace?" Anahita asked slowly.

"A particularly powerful djinn built it. He served Aladdin for a time, but now he is free."

Dread curled around Anahita's heart. "Djinn

are dangerous. Especially powerful ones. A djinn was responsible for the wells drying up in Tasnim. They grant wishes with no thought as to the consequences, and do not care to repair the damage they cause. If a djinn built this palace, then there is surely trouble coming. Where did he get the building materials, the artisans…you cannot trust a djinn!"

Maram's smile only widened. "I trust this one. He was a friend of my mother's. He would not make trouble for me, and now he is free…I trust him even more. Not all djinn are troublemakers. It is their masters who make the trouble, Amani told me, for djinn are slaves to their masters' will."

Philemon's words on the way to Tasnim began to make sense. "So if a djinn's former master said the ruin of Tasnim was his fault, then…"

Maram shrugged. "He's probably right. But Tasnim is not ruined – it's merely deserted. Locked up and hard to get into, Aladdin said."

"I've seen it," Anahita said. "He's right. But now the water has returned to the wells, the people can return, and Philemon…"

"He's handsome, your Philemon. What sort of lover is he?" Maram demanded.

Anahita felt her cheeks grow hot. "I…I…have little to compare him to, but…I think…he is…a fine lover…" Anahita broke off at Maram's laughter.

"You mean he truly is your lover? Ah, never have I been so mistaken. First I thought him the sheikh, then another lovesick eunuch to join the others…I am sorry I tried to seduce him." Maram looked suitably contrite, before her gaze turned thoughtful. "Though I have never been threatened at swordpoint to stop seducing a man. Usually they don't want me to stop. Instead, he grabbed you and professed his love for you. You've caught a strange one, there, Ana. Does he have other peculiarities, perhaps?"

She should never have drawn her blades. Not on Philemon. He'd been defending her, defending their love. "I told him to go away." Anahita burst into tears. "He said he loved me and I sent him away!"

"But he didn't go far. I've known a lot of men, and if he'd wanted to leave you, he would have. He'll come to find you, soon enough. Perhaps you should head home to Father's palace, and wash away the travel dust so that you can greet him properly when he does." She glanced toward the garden. "Aladdin will keep him occupied until then."

Her husband. Philemon. Tasnim. Anahita grasped Maram's arm. "But Philemon is the real Prince of Tasnim, and he thinks your husband is an imposter, pretending to be him. He wanted to kill him!"

Maram paled. "Then go. I will broker a peace between them. Diplomacy is my strength, after all. Wash, rest, and wait!" She ordered some guards to take Anahita to the palace, before hurrying out to the garden.

Anahita longed to stay, but short of fighting her way through Maram's men — a feat she doubted she'd manage without Haidar and Asad to help her — she had little choice but to go home with them, and hope her sister was right.

Maram was rarely wrong…but if this was the one time, Anahita might never see Philemon again. She prayed her sister had not lost her touch with men, or diplomacy. For Anahita's heart depended on both.

Forty-Four

Philemon took a deep breath as he surveyed the Sultan's audience chamber. He knew this was just a formality, for the Sultan's matchmaker had agreed to the marriage long before he turned frog, but that didn't stop his heart from leaping into his throat in fear if something went wrong.

But it would not. He was a prince – a true prince, unlike Aladdin – and a fitting husband for any princess. Or so he told himself.

A commotion at the gate told him Aladdin's servants had arrived, with his gift. The crowd parted, waves of an ancient sea at the command of a prophet. Or a prince.

"A gift to the Sultan from His Royal Highness, Prince Philemon of Tasnim!" the door guardian djinn – Kaveh – roared, his voice perfectly pitched to resonate through the hall.

Not for the first time, Philemon regretted losing the loyalty of the ancient vizier. But he didn't have time to dwell on it.

"Where is this prince?" the Sultan demanded. "Tell him to show his face, so that I may thank him for such a handsome gift."

It was identical to what he'd received from Aladdin in exchange for permission to marry Maram, even down to the livery of the servants. The Sultan was not fool enough to refuse it.

But Philemon was not Aladdin – he needed no fanfare or parade to announce his presence. A true prince commanded attention, or he did not deserve his crown.

Philemon strode into the archway that marked the boundary between the dim throne room and the dazzling desert daylight. He stood in the light, silhouetted against the morning sun. "I am here. I have come to claim my bride, a daughter of the Sultan to become the new Princess of Tasnim."

The crowd buzzed, but they did not hinder his march toward the dais where the Sultan sat.

When Philemon reached the row of prostrate servants presenting their gifts of gold and jewels, he stopped and bowed. Just low enough for his eyes to meet those of the seated Sultan.

The Sultan looked shaken.

Because of Aladdin, Philemon guessed.

"When I saw how happy my younger half-brother, Aladdin, was with his wife, I refused to wait any longer. I must marry, and it must be one of your daughters," Philemon continued.

If this didn't work, Philemon vowed he'd force Aladdin to confess the truth at the point of his sword, no matter what his witch of a wife wanted.

In the shadows behind the Sultan's throne, a woman leaned forward and whispered something into the Sultan's ear. He gave the slightest nod, then rose.

"This audience is at an end for today. I will hear more petitions on the morrow. I will meet privately with the Prince of Tasnim," the Sultan announced.

The court slowly emptied, until the golden doors closed with a clunk of finality.

Only then did the woman step out of the shadows. Her gown, which Philemon had taken for plain black, glittered in the light, for the wine-coloured linen was embroidered with jewels.

The Sultan did not miss Philemon's interest in the mysterious woman. "If you wish to discuss marriage, my matchmaker must be present. She knows which of my daughters are suitable."

Philemon nodded. The woman hadn't been so richly dressed when he last met her, but it made sense to have her there. Though he would be the judge of who was suitable, not her.

The matchmaker led the way into the palace proper, choosing a chamber that was better suited to an intimate discussion than the audience hall. One more richly furnished than the place where he'd first met with the woman, if indeed this was the same one. For the matchmaker he'd met here before hadn't swished her hips quite that seductively as she walked. Nor had she been the first to sit on the floor cushions, as this one did.

She'd surprised the Sultan, too, Philemon noticed, hiding his grin.

Philemon and the Sultan took their seats and servants brought in refreshments, before departing at a signal from the matchmaker. This door clicked shut so quietly Philemon was barely aware of it.

The woman threw off her veil and reached for a cup of wine.

Maram. Her haughty brows furrowed when she found both men staring at her. "He's family, Father. Aladdin's brother. Perhaps if we find him a wife, he'll learn to stop staring at women's faces when he is fortunate enough to see one." She sipped from her wine cup, then shot a red-lipped smile in Philemon's direction. "If my brother-in-law can tell us what he wants in a wife, perhaps I can help him."

"I want Anahita," he blurted out, closing his eyes to better resist the spell she seemed to cast simply by looking at him.

The Sultan cleared his throat. "My daughter Anahita is in mourning, for she has only recently been widowed. It will be some time before she is ready to wed again, if ever."

"And the daughter of a mere concubine – hardly fitting for such an important prince," Maram interjected. "I am sure one of Mahsa, the Moon Queen's daughters, would be far better suited. She has two daughters of marriageable age – Katayun and Mahvash. Mahvash is the image of her mother – sweet and obedient, and likely just as fertile. Katayun has been well trained by her mother in the practicalities of running a harem, and well able to keep your other wives and concubines in order. I have heard tales that the Prince of Tasnim's harem rivals my father's own, and a young, virile man like yourself without an heir…"

"I want Anahita," Philemon repeated. "I want her as my wife, and no one else. Now." He wished the woman wasn't here – her very presence set his teeth on edge, and made him most irritable. Left alone with the Sultan, he would not have announced his desire so directly, nor demanded it. There would have been conversation, negotiation…but the witch wanted him to fail. Why else would she be making this so difficult?

"But her husband has only just died," Maram snapped, eyeing him with considerable irritation.

If he failed, he'd get his harem garden back…but what use was it without Anahita? What use was anything without her?

Last night, Maram had insisted if he followed her plan, he would win Anahita back. Now, it was as though last night had never happened. Or was this woman one of Maram's sisters, identical in appearance to Maram, but not the same person?

If she wasn't Maram, then he had nothing to fear from her.

Philemon rose to his feet. "I am her husband, by the laws of the desert people. Sheikh Basit's death frightened her, and she refused to be left alone. She shared my tent that night, and the marriage was sealed by a wedding breakfast at dawn the next day. I will not leave the city until you return my wife to me!"

A wicked smile appeared on the woman's face, which dissolved into a shocked expression as quickly as it had appeared. "But one of the Sultan's virtuous daughters would not...could not..."

It was Philemon's turn to smile. "She already carries my child. And the child will be born in Tasnim, as the heir to the principality should be!" It was possible, therefore not entirely a lie.

Maram's eyes danced with mischief – for this woman could be no one else. "How do you know it is not Sheikh Basit's baby in her belly?"

Philemon drew himself up. "Because I slew the man myself before the consummation could occur."

"You killed him?" The Sultan stared.

If Philemon had ever doubted Anahita was her father's assassin, the doubts died then and there. "He encroached on Tasnim's territory, attacking towns that were under my protection, and we do not treat such things lightly." Philemon allowed the Sultan a small smile. "I'm sure if you were in my position, you would have done the same."

The Sultan looked thoughtful for a moment, before turning to Maram. "Fetch her," he commanded.

Maram obeyed.

Once the door had shut behind her, the Sultan poured himself a cup of wine and gestured for Philemon to do the same. "I had heard that Tasnim's wells ran dry."

Philemon's mouth was drier. "They did, but the waters have returned, sweeter and more plentiful than ever," he managed to say. He poured, then drank. "Tasnim is a worthy ally for anyone who wishes to travel and trade across the desert."

"So it is. But what if you were to suffer some misfortune? Who would be the ruler of Tasnim then?" the Sultan asked.

"The city will pass to the child my wife carries," Philemon said slowly.

"A child cannot hold a city, especially an

unborn one. Surely your brother would inherit instead."

Brother? Oh, Aladdin.

"Hence my need for a wife. One who has proven fertile already," Philemon managed to say, feigning nonchalance to cover the chill that had crept over his heart. Did the Sultan intend to have him assassinated so that Aladdin could steal the city?

But the Sultan's assassin was…

"Ah, Anahita. Good. I have some questions for you, child," the Sultan said.

Anahita stood awkwardly before the closed door, staring at her father. "Yes, Father?"

"Who killed Sheikh Basit?" the Sultan demanded.

Anahita wet her lips. "Why, Prince Philemon, of course. It was terrifying to see him strike the blow. Ask anyone in Basit's camp."

The Sultan seemed surprised, then relieved.

Because his daughter hadn't killed a man?

No, because Philemon didn't know that she had, Philemon decided.

"Are you carrying his child?"

Philemon closed his eyes.

Forty-Five

"Are you carrying his child?" the Sultan repeated.

Anahita shot a dark glance at Maram. Damn her spies. "Yes," Anahita admitted. "The midwife confirmed it this morning."

Philemon's child, not Basit's, but she could not tell her father that. Nor Philemon, while her father was listening.

"Take the girl, then," the Sultan said. "I wish you well of her."

Philemon rose and took her arm. "Thank you."

Anahita found herself in the corridor with Philemon. "What are you – " she began

"You are my wife, and I am taking you home," he interrupted, heading down the corridor as though he knew where he was going.

Anahita wrenched free. "What are you doing? The harem's that way, and even if my father has given me to you like some bauble, he will not let you have any of his own wives and concubines."

"Then how do we get out of this palace?" Philemon looked bewildered.

Anahita took pity on him. "This way," she said. Behind her, she heard the familiar footsteps of Haidar and Asad as they followed her, and she breathed a sigh of relief. No matter what her father said, she would never be some prince's plaything.

"If you know the way to a good inn, that would help, too," Philemon said softly, glancing around.

"Asad will know the best," she said. "But I have apartments here in the palace, and my sister Maram – "

"Has spies everywhere," Philemon finished.

A flash of understanding sparked between them. "Asad will lead the way, and Haidar will make sure we are not followed," Anahita said.

The two men moved into place, setting a steady pace that moved easily through the busy streets. Philemon was stiff and agitated at her side, but he didn't say another word until they were behind the closed door of the best room in what Asad insisted was the most prestigious inn in the city.

"Your father and your sister want you to kill me, so her husband can have Tasnim," Philemon said. He pulled his knife from its sheath and flipped it so it lay hilt-first in his hand. "Take it and use it now. I would rather die at this very moment than to be stabbed in the back when I believed I was happy."

Anahita stared at the knife, and then him, in horror. "I don't know of any such plan. Maram would never want Tasnim, for it is too isolated for her. She'd be bored without harem and court politics to play with."

"The Sultan made it clear he wants my city. He wanted to know all about the succession, should some misfortune befall me!"

Anahita touched her belly. "How did you know about the baby? Even I didn't know for sure until this morning."

"I guessed! I lied! I don't know!" Philemon exploded. "He wasn't going to let me marry you…and then, suddenly, he changed his mind and handed you to me. Like merchants trade their daughters for Tasnim's hospitality. I would have carried you to the city as its princess, a ruler who would sit at my side, but not like this." He thrust the knife at her, hilt-first. "Do it! If you are truly his assassin, cut out my heart. For it cannot hurt as much as it does now, knowing the woman I love will kill me." He tore open his shirt, baring his breast.

Anahita seized the knife and flung it, point down, into the floor. "I will not!" she said fiercely. "I am not my father's assassin! I killed men who deserved their fate – animals who would have killed me, given the chance. You are not like them, and I will not help anyone who tries to take Tasnim from you!"

He was the one talking of heartache, yet hers felt like it was ready to break. Her father has used her as a pawn to destroy his enemies, but she would no longer play politics. That was Maram's world, not hers. And if Maram could marry…so could she.

She stared into Philemon's eyes. "Marry me," she said. "And then take me home to Tasnim with you."

He dropped his gaze and her heart sank with it.

"Please," she begged, then kissed him.

The fire built between them, burning as bright as their first kiss. He wanted her — Anahita knew that. But then why…?

He set his hands on her shoulders and broke the kiss. "I cannot marry you, because we are already married." His eyes begged her to understand.

She shook her head. "We can't be. I'd remember."

Still he didn't smile. "By the laws of the desert people, when a couple share a tent for the night and share a morning meal afterward, they are married. The night Sheikh Basit died…" He shook his head. "In the panic of that night, I forgot what I should have known.

And with you in my arms…I lost my mind entirely. You are everything I ever wished for in a wife, and more. I should have left you alone that night, but I could not resist you."

Memories of that first night brought a blush to Anahita's cheeks. She had not been able to resist him, either, nor had she wanted to. As for letting her sleep in that tent alone…Anahita had begged him to stay when he'd suggested leaving. Realisation dawned. "That's how we broke the curse." The very night she'd vowed to do anything Philemon needed to break it, she already had.

"Perhaps. It was my first curse, and, I hope, my last." Philemon drew in a deep breath. "So…you aren't angry at me for wedding you without you being aware of it? Without asking for your consent to the match?" He rushed to continue before she could respond. "If you are, say the word and I will divorce you, though it would break my heart to do so. I could not force you into a match you do not desire."

"No, you wouldn't." She remembered the passion of that first night, and every night after. Until last night's loneliness, not knowing if she would ever see him again. "I came to you willingly, Philemon. Every night since, and so I intend to continue. Together, with you. No talk of divorce or cutting out hearts. I am your wife. I am your *wife*." The word tasted good on her lips.

"My one and only." Now his smile appeared, and it was blindingly bright. His arms slid around her, pulling her close. His kiss held the promise of everything she'd ever wanted.

She laid her head against his bare chest, where his heartbeat thrummed under her cheek. "Take me home to Tasnim, my Frog Prince."

"Anything for the princess who saved me."

Forty-Six

"Here she is, Your Highness," a man's voice said. Not Haidar or Asad.

Anahita settled Vega on her glove and turned to face the newcomer.

She had to look up to meet the eyes of a tall woman in purple. Even her eyes were that unusual colour.

"Who is this?" Anahita asked coolly.

The bowing servant straightened, and she was surprised to see he wore nothing but a loincloth, like some lowly slave.

"I am Lord Kaveh, once the Grand Vizier

of Tasnim, now slave to the ring that was once the prince's ring of office. My magic still runs strong through these tunnels, and the doors still open to my touch. I serve Prince Aladdin now," the man said smoothly.

The man who had made the jewelled gardens, Anahita remembered. But that did not give him the right to intrude in her private chambers. She'd set Vega on him if he woke the baby.

"I meant the woman."

He bowed again, even lower and more elaborately this time. "Your Highness, Princess Zuleika the Enchantress, Mistress of Beacon Isle, may I present Her Highness, Princess Anahita, the Princess of Tasnim?"

Anahita stared. This was the woman who had cursed Philemon and the city? She didn't look a day older than Anahita herself, and…was she pregnant? Philemon had never said anything about her being a princess, either. This wasn't the witch she'd imagined at all.

Zuleika inclined her head. "I heard that people were returning to Tasnim, now their prince had been found. There was even talk about the wells refilling. I had to see this for myself. Particularly the princess who could fall in love with a frog."

"He was never truly a frog. He didn't talk like one. And no frog has ever attacked one of my hunting falcons the way he did," Anahita said.

The enchantress closed her eyes. "Ah, you are a witch, then. Your magic is faint, but I see it now. That must be useful. Even I would have to bespell the bird for it to sit as contently as yours does. Especially underground."

"She has the freedom of the air and light wells whenever she wishes. So does Merlin, though she prefers to fish in the wells beneath the city, for she is fond of frogs. All my birds are free to come and go as they wish. I do not believe in enslaving anyone." Anahita sniffed. "I would not expect some barbarian king's daughter to understand."

Zuleika's eyes snapped open. "I am the daughter of an enchantress, not some king or prince. But I married one, and this one will be king when his uncle dies." She patted her belly. Definitely pregnant. "I have seen more of the world — and of slavery — than you ever will, daughter of the desert. I think if more women ruled this world than the foolish men who mess it up now, we might see an end to such things. But I cannot turn all of them into frogs, so it will not be in my lifetime." She smiled sadly.

Frogs or corpses — what was worse? Fakhri, Basit and their ilk would never trouble the world again, while frogs could be redeemed. Or maybe Philemon was unique in that. "It will take more than one woman to change the world. This city is enough for me," Anahita said. This girl…woman…whatever she was, was more like Maram than Anahita. One who played at politics, who had more power than Anahita could ever want.

"Keeping the Prince of Tasnim from drying up the city's wells through more foolishness is certainly enough to keep any woman busy," Zuleika said.

"At least nothing a good storm can't fix," Anahita said, thinking of what Asad had told her about the rivers that ran below the desert dunes. A wail rose from the next room. Mirza was awake. She sighed. "And teach my son to be better."

Zuleika nodded. "You should know Philemon promised me a great deal of gold for helping him. Gold which is still in your treasury, for he refused to pay me. I have no need of it now, so you may keep it. Consider it a wedding gift, or a wager, if you will, for I never thought there would be a woman willing to do what you have. Loving a frog – ha! Even my husband would not believe it. Wait until I tell him."

Anahita opened her mouth to thank her for her generosity, but the enchantress had vanished. So had the djinn.

Anahita tended to Mirza and fed him until he fell asleep, but the enchantress did not return.

And all was well in Tasnim, safe beneath the desert sands, where the wells never ran dry again.

About the Author

Demelza Carlton has always loved the ocean, but on her first snorkelling trip she found she was afraid of fish.

She has since swum with sea lions, sharks and sea cucumbers and stood on spray drenched cliffs over a seething sea as a seven-metre cyclonic swell surged in, shattering a shipwreck below.

Demelza now lives in Perth, Western Australia, the shark attack capital of the world.

The *Ocean's Gift* series was her first foray into fiction, followed by her suspense thriller *Nightmares* trilogy. She swears the *Mel Goes to Hell* series ambushed her on a crowded train and wouldn't leave her alone.

Want to know more? You can follow Demelza on Facebook, Twitter, YouTube or her website, Demelza Carlton's Place at:

www.demelzacarlton.com

Books by Demelza Carlton

Siren of Secrets series
Ocean's Secret (#1)
Ocean's Gift (#2)
Ocean's Infiltrator (#3)

Siren of War series
Ocean's Justice (#1)
Ocean's Widow (#2)
Ocean's Bride (#3)
Ocean's Rise (#4)
Ocean's War (#5)
How To Catch Crabs

Nightmares Trilogy
Nightmares of Caitlin Lockyer (#1)
Necessary Evil of Nathan Miller (#2)
Afterlife of Alana Miller (#3)

Mel Goes to Hell series
Welcome to Hell (#1)
See You in Hell (#2)
Mel Goes to Hell (#3)
To Hell and Back (#4)
The Holiday From Hell (#5)
All Hell Breaks Loose (#6)

Romance Island Resort series

Maid for the Rock Star (#1)
The Rock Star's Email Order Bride (#2)
The Rock Star's Virginity (#3)
The Rock Star and the Billionaire (#4)
The Rock Star Wants A Wife (#5)
The Rock Star's Wedding (#6)
Maid for the South Pole (#7)
Jailbird Bride (#8)

Romance a Medieval Fairytale series

Enchant: Beauty and the Beast Retold
Dance: Cinderella Retold
Fly: Goose Girl Retold
Revel: Twelve Dancing Princesses Retold
Silence: Little Mermaid Retold
Awaken: Sleeping Beauty Retold
Embellish: Brave Little Tailor Retold
Appease: Princess and the Pea Retold
Blow: Three Little Pigs Retold
Return: Hansel and Gretel Retold
Wish: Aladdin Retold
Melt: Snow Queen Retold
Spin: Rumpelstiltskin Retold
Kiss: Frog Prince Retold
Hunt: Red Riding Hood Retold
Reflect: Snow White Retold
Roar: Goldilocks Retold
Cobble: Elves and the Shoemaker Retold